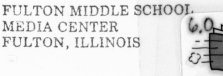

Three Lives to Live

ANNE LINDBERGH

A MINSTREL® BOOK

PUBLISHED BY POCKET BOOKS

New York   London   Toronto   Sydney   Tokyo   Singapore

A Minstrel Book published by
POCKET BOOKS, a division of Simon & Schuster Inc.
1230 Avenue of the Americas, New York, NY 10020

Copyright © 1992 by Anne Lindbergh

Published by arrangement with Little, Brown and Company

ISBN: 0-671-86732-6

First Minstrel Books printing May 1995

10 9 8 7 6 5 4 3 2 1

A MINSTREL BOOK and colophon are registered trademarks
of Simon & Schuster Inc.

Cover art by Robert Sauber

Printed in the U.S.A.

For Anne, my mother,
and Constance, my daughter —
a book about choices

Hot off the Press:
The Only Authorized
Autobiography
of

Garet Atkins,
7-B

Whetstone Academy for Girls
Mrs. Magorian's 3rd Period
English Class

Footnote: (dictated by Mrs. Magorian)

auto- from the Greek *autos* (self)
bio- from the Greek *bios* (life)
-graphy from the Greek *graphos* (written)

Autobiography:
The story of one's life, written by oneself.

Chapter 1
(First Draft)

The story of my life, written by myself? Who is she trying to kid? At best, this will be the story of my life as Mrs. Magorian thinks I ought to write it. I'll give you the truth and nothing but the truth, but don't expect the whole truth. At least, not unless Mrs. Magorian gets sick and we have an open-minded substitute.

Here goes: My life was a happy one until last week when Daisy got her laptop computer. Though if I'd been smart, I would have guessed my happy days were over back in September, when Daisy got her learning disability. Of course, it didn't occur to Daisy to become learning disabled until she got her canopy bed last August. So let's just say that my troubles began in July, when I got my twin sister, Daisy.

(Mrs. Magorian says I have to start over. She says this is supposed to be my story, not Daisy's. There's no way it will be the whole truth without Daisy in it. But I warned you, right?)

3

Chapter 1
(Second Draft)

Riddle: When is a sister no longer a sister?
Answer: When you desist her. (I wish!) Get it?

(Mrs. Magorian says this won't do either.
She says you can desist an action, but not a
person. She also says that The Professional
Author would allow his readers to draw their
own conclusion about Daisy.)

4

Chapter 1
(Third Draft)

The girls in 7-B are writing autobiographies for SWAP, which stands for Student Writing Achievement Project. Next month, a famous author is going to judge the project and give out prizes. We don't know which author because the headmistress hasn't found one yet who wants to do it. Meanwhile, everyone in school is writing something, but only 7-B gets to use the school computers. How did we luck out? Because the girls in 7-B are supposed to be bad writers. At least not as good writers as the girls in 7-A.

Which happens to be totally untrue. I may be a messy writer. It may take me longer to write in cursive than it takes Daisy, for example. But I'm a lot faster than Daisy on a keyboard, and I have a whole lot more to say. I told Mrs. Magorian this, but all she said was, "That's nice, Garet. Your autobiography will give you a chance to prove it."

Why are we writing autobiographies instead of stories or poems like the rest of the school? Because according to Mrs. Magorian, we're not only bad writers, we're also uninspired writers.

"If you write about yourselves, at least you'll never run out of subject matter," she explained. Then she switched to her preachy voice and added, "Remember, you only have one life to live! It won't hurt you to take an honest look at it. Will it, now, girls?"

"When I look at my life, all I see is Daisy," I informed her. "Daisy has a cute little trick of occupying center stage — haven't you noticed? Besides, I owe it to the world to reveal her deep, dark secrets. Who is she? Where did she come from? How long does she intend to stay?"

"I'm more concerned with your own deep, dark secrets," Mrs. Magorian said.

I warned her that my life was dull as dishwater, but she just switched to her preachy voice again and said that any observant human being should be able to list three interesting things that happen to him every day. By "him," she meant me.

"Breakfast, lunch, and dinner?" I suggested.

The other girls thought this was funny. Mrs. Magorian did not. "We should eat to live, not live to eat," she said. Then she looked me straight in the eye and told me she hoped I'd rise above my obsession with food and have the courage to show her a little of the real Garet Atkins.

"If you want reality, how come I have to leave Daisy out of it?" I asked.

Mrs. Magorian said it was my life, not Daisy's.

6

Funny, that's exactly what I told my grandmother after Daisy fell off the canopy bed last August.

My exact words happen to have been, "It's my life, isn't it?" and my grandmother's answer was, "Daisy is *part* of your life now."

I tried it on Mrs. Magorian: "Daisy is part of my life now!" Mrs. Magorian's answer was, "Daisy can write her own autobiography." But Daisy is in 7-A.

Question: Why is Daisy in 7-A if she has a learning disability?

Answer: She faked the learning disability — that's why.

But I'm going to save Daisy's fake learning disability for later because Mrs. Magorian says The Professional Author keeps his reader's interest by creating an aura of suspense.

She also says that to get the reader's interest in the first place, The Professional Author introduces his main character in an offbeat way. My main character is me, but I can't just write, "My name is Garet Atkins, I have brown hair and hazel eyes, I'm thirteen, and I deserve my own computer." Mrs. Magorian says this kind of introduction is too conventional. She says to read some really good books and notice the subtle ways that characters are introduced. She says I'll find some useful gimmicks. I already know those gimmicks. One of them goes like this:

A slim, mature-looking girl walked past Computer Shack without casting a glance at the laptop model her grandmother didn't give her for her thirteenth birthday because she gave it to her twin sister, Daisy, instead.

The next store window had a mirror. The slim, mature-looking girl stopped to look in it so she could wipe the crystal tears off her cheek. The face she saw in the mirror wasn't as pretty as Daisy's face, but it showed a lot more character. It had brown hair cut an inch above her ear on one side and an inch below on the other. It had hazel eyes. It was her own face.

She also saw that she forgot to change out of her barf-green gym suit, so she could read the name tape in the mirror. It said, SNIKTA TERAG.

Mrs. Magorian just walked down my row and paused when she got to me. She says to try writing my autobiography the way she says to do it instead of telling all the ways she says not to do it.

Mrs. Magorian also says to stop saying what Mrs. Magorian says.

Chapter 1
(Final Draft)

Like I wrote before I was so rudely interrupted,
I've led a happy life. I was born on October 29, 1980.
Until Daisy turned up, the only bad thing that happened to me was the death of my parents when I was
two, which hardly counts because I don't remember.
Ever since then, I've lived with Gratkins in her big
old-fashioned house that was built a century ago.
Gratkins (short for Grandmother Atkins) was born in
that house in 1930, long before our crowded neighborhood grew up around it. She had eight brothers
and sisters, so the house is used to children.

I'm used to my grandmother, if it comes to that.
I've always rated her way above my friends' parents.
At least I did until Daisy came into the picture and
things began to change. So how *did* Daisy come into
the picture? Mrs. Magorian says it's high time I told
you. She came down the laundry chute — that's how.

Most houses don't have a laundry chute, but most
houses aren't like ours. Our house has nine bedrooms,
more closets than I'd care to count, and miles of

corridor. Gratkins and I only use a fraction of that space. Back when she was a kid, it was a different story. Apart from her huge family, there was also a live-in cook, plus a maid named Lena.

According to Gratkins, when Lena wasn't waiting on table, she washed clothes in the cellar. The way the clothes got there was down the laundry chute. All my great-grandmother had to do was lift this wooden flap and drop them in. When the chute was installed, it was considered a labor-saving device. If you ask me, it didn't save much labor for Lena. But people back then thought it was pretty cool. You can tell by the writing on the flap:

BE FIFTY YEARS AHEAD OF YOUR TIME!
ACME SUPERIOR HOUSEHOLD PRODUCTS
GIVE YOU A NEW LEASE ON LIFE!

The chute is a thing of the past now, for two reasons. In the first place, we do our wash in the Sears washer and dryer in the kitchen. In the second place, my great-grandparents nailed the flap shut when Gratkins was thirteen. I asked why, but Gratkins wouldn't say. She believes it's rude to ask people questions about their past. I happen to disagree, but that's beside the point. The point is, how did Daisy get in?

Since I don't know, I'll tell you instead how she got out. It happened during a heat wave last July. I woke up grouchy, and my temper didn't improve as the day grew hotter. Gratkins finally ordered me to take a book down to the cellar to cool off. Our cellar has thick stone walls with dusty slits of windows up near the ceiling that the sun can barely filter through. It's cool, but it's also damp and crawling with spiders. Gratkins meant business, though, so I went down.

"Try the laundry room!" she called after me. "There used to be a good bright light in there, over the sink."

There still was. And by a miracle the sink was spider-free, so I climbed in. It was fairly comfortable as long as I scrunched around the faucets. I was peacefully reading when I heard a noise like an indoor avalanche. I looked up, and with my own eyes I saw a girl come skidding out of the laundry chute and land flat on her back, in what seemed like a mess of peach-colored tissue paper but turned out to be her dress. She was pale, and too scared to talk.

Not me, though. I was firing questions at her before she had time to catch her breath. Who was she, and how did she get into our laundry chute? It starts in the second-floor linen closet, just outside my room. What was she doing up there? And why was she wearing dress-up clothes? In her gauzy dress with a sash on her behind and smocking on her front, she looked like a little girl at a birthday party. Except for two things: she was my age, and she was covered with spiderwebs.

Strange? Not as strange as the fact that Gratkins didn't ask her anything at all. When I brought the girl upstairs she just smiled and said, "Why, hello, Daisy!"

I'll never forget how surprised that girl looked. I

11

was surprised, too. "What is this?" I demanded. "Have you two met before?"

The girl shook her head. Gratkins said, "You ask too many questions."

She told me that Daisy's past was her own private business, and I had to quit prying into it. What Gratkins says goes, so I tried to keep my mouth shut. Even when we took Daisy in to live with us. Even when Gratkins told people that Daisy was my sister. Don't get the idea that I was happy, though. The truth is, I was furious! Not that I had anything personal against Daisy — not at first, anyway. It's just that Gratkins and I had become kind of a couple, and as the saying goes, three's a crowd.

It was the sisters business that bothered me the most. In my opinion, it was a mistake. Since Daisy was obviously my age, people assumed we were twins. Gratkins had to agree. What else could she do? All the same, I think she should have consulted me. It's not so terrific having a twin sister, because people compare you all the time. If I had any choice in the matter, I'd have a brother instead.

"I'm not asking a question," I told Gratkins. "I just want it on record that I wish I knew why Daisy has to be my sister."

She said, "You look like sisters — that's why."

She's right. Daisy has the same color hair as me, and the same eyes, and the exact same dimple in her chin. That's as far as the resemblance goes, however. Daisy is skinny, and a little shorter, and has long hair. She's also prettier. But the main thing is that she doesn't behave like me. I pointed this out to the kids at school, but they said it wasn't surprising. They said naturally Daisy wouldn't behave like me since we'd been brought up separately until we were nearly thirteen. Then they'd want to know why we were separated. Daisy wouldn't breathe a word about her past, so I had to come up with a good story. The best I could think of was that after our parents died, we were split up between two sets of grandparents.

"How come you never told us about her?" the kids would ask. "Pretty sneaky, Garet!"

I had an answer for that one: "Would you talk about your twin sister if she was as weird as Daisy?"

Because face it — there's something weird about Daisy. How come Gratkins knew her, but she didn't know Gratkins?

And how come she knew her way around? In our house, that's not easy. Some of my friends still get lost, but not Daisy. She knew where the bathroom was, and the way to the back stairs. Our back stairs are so hard to find that they almost count as secret.

On the other hand, the stuff that was *in* the house really freaked her out: the microwave oven for instance, and the television set. She spent the first evening switching channels with the remote control. Since then, she's been hooked. It makes no difference what she watches: soaps, sports, commercials — she loves it all. TV is what finally convinced her that I looked like other kids. At first, she got such a kick out of my clothes and my hairstyle that it was insulting. "Your hair is that way on purpose?" she kept asking. "And honestly nobody laughs?"

But as I said, I had nothing against her at first.

13

Except maybe for the way Gratkins spoiled her. Which brings me back to the canopy bed. We shared my bedroom for the first few weeks. Gratkins put an extra mattress on my floor and we took turns sleeping on it, which was fun. But then Gratkins said life wasn't one long slumber party and Daisy should have her own room.

Now, when I wrote that we live in a big, old-fashioned house, I didn't say a big, *rich* old-fashioned house. Not that it looks poor either. It just looks empty. In most of those nine bedrooms, there's not a stick of furniture. Gratkins had to sell off the antiques before she could afford my tuition at Whetstone. In other words, the problem wasn't so much a room for Daisy as a bed to put in it.

"I'll have to buy one," said Gratkins. She sounded worried, but nowhere near as worried as when she remembered the Academy. "I'd better go have a talk with the headmistress while I'm out. I'm afraid this means double the tuition, come fall."

I saw no cause for worry. "Can't Daisy go to Whetstone Junior High?"

She gave me a cold look. "If anyone switches to public school, it should be you. You've led a privileged life up to this day. Daisy has been less fortunate."

"How do you know?" I asked.

Gratkins scowled at me. "No questions!"

"Why not?" I asked. "Why is it rude to ask about the past? If other people thought like you, there'd be no history!"

She didn't answer, so I took advantage of her silence to suggest switching us both to public school.

"Not on your life!" Gratkins snapped. "Not even if it means mortgaging the house."

I knew she'd say no. When she was growing up, she went the whole way through the public school system wishing she could wear a barf-green gym suit with her name tape on the pocket. Her parents couldn't afford to send her to the Academy because of all those brothers and sisters. I would have been thrilled to save her some money by switching to Whetstone Junior High, but did I get a chance? Dream on, Garet!

My last hope was that Daisy would back me up, but Daisy had her heart set on the Academy. She didn't even change her mind once she got there. She settled right in, and wouldn't you know it — after just one day of classes, she got moved to 7-A. It's bad enough having a twin sister who's prettier than you are. Try having one who's smarter than you are, too! It was the unfair combination of smart and pretty that got Daisy the canopy bed.

By now you're supposed to be itching to know the story of the canopy bed. I've mentioned it several times already. Mrs. Magorian says this is called foreshadowing, and it's something The Professional Author does in case you're too dumb to guess what's going to be important in his book. That bed is important all right, and now I'll tell you why.

(When Mrs. Magorian read this she said, "That's better, Garet. See what you can do when you make an effort?")

Chapter 2

I was right when I said this would be the story of my life as Mrs. Magorian thinks I ought to write it. After four beginnings, I was hoping to get down to business. But she says first I have to put in a flashback.

Even the writers in 7-B know that a flashback is when you ruin a good story by stopping to tell about something that happened earlier. I find this a little tedious, but authors do it anyway. In order not to confuse you, they put their flashbacks in italic print. (That's the slanty one.) The Whetstone Academy computers can't handle italics. Daisy's laptop will, but Daisy isn't in a lending mood. Who cares?

When I finish my autobiography, I'll send it to a publisher. It will be a best-seller, and the book flap will say, "Ms. Atkins wrote this masterpiece on a lousy school computer. Her sister had her own laptop, but she refused to lend it."

My readers will ask, "Garet Atkins has a sister? What's she like?"

And people in the know will say, "Daisy is prettier and smarter, but otherwise she's kind of blah."

So I'd better get my flashback over with, or I'll be trapped forever in chapter two.

Mrs. Magorian says that knowing how to slide gracefully in and out of a flashback is a sign of The Professional Author, so it's good practice to put one in our autobiographies. She also says that a flashback should pivot on a useful gimmick such as the scent of a rose or a familiar old tune that takes you back in time. Mine is shepherd's pie.

Ready? First imagine me: slim, mature-looking thirteen-year-old Garet. I'm sitting at a Whetstone Academy computer. My mind is partly on my work, but mostly on my lunch. Lunch isn't until after Health and Hygiene, but a nasty smell is already penetrating the computer room. I'm praying it isn't road kill. The Academy boasts about delicious, nutritious cafeteria meals, but it's a well-known fact that the headmistress gets our meat straight off the nearest interstate. Sometimes it's crow, and sometimes it's cat. I suspect there's an occasional skunk. We had road kill yesterday, but that doesn't mean we won't have it again today served up as shepherd's road-kill pie.

Shepherd's pie! Gratkins made shepherd's pie for supper the night I found out about Daisy's canopy bed. It was back in August, when I was still twelve.

So now imagine me eating in the kitchen. Why the kitchen? Because the dining room doesn't have a table — that's why. It has floor-to-ceiling windows and a chandelier, but Gratkins sold the table to buy our VCR. Which is why I'm at the kitchen table eating shepherd's pie. It would be a while yet before I grew slim and mature looking. Meanwhile, I liked mashed potatoes a whole lot more than meat. Even when the meat was cow, not crow. But Gratkins believes in eating everything on your plate, so the next thing you have to imagine is me feeling nauseated.

I had one thing going for me: Daisy's attitude toward food. She's finicky. I don't mean she has no appetite. She eats like a horse, in spite of being skinny. But nothing on her plate is allowed to touch anything else on her plate. If we have lima beans and corn, they have to be served in separate piles, and they have to stay that way. Even when they come as succotash, Daisy divides them up. Then she chews and swallows a mouthful of beans before she lets her fork so much as touch the corn. I tell her it turns into succotash again in her stomach, but she does it anyway.

That evening last August, I was grateful for Daisy's attitude. It was easy to convince her that life would be simpler if she had all meat and I had all potatoes. We were negotiating a trade when Gratkins brought up the question of the bed.

I remember the doting way she reached over and tugged on Daisy's ponytail. "How about it, Daisy? Have you made up your mind?"

"Made up her mind about what?" I asked.

Daisy batted her lashes and simpered at her plate. She was performing surgery on the shepherd's pie. By the time she finished, no one would guess the meat and potatoes had started out together. Unfortunately, the potatoes lost their appeal as they grew cold.

18

"About what?" I repeated.

Gratkins answered for her. "Daisy is moving into her own bedroom, remember? So she has to hurry up and choose a bed."

I wasn't too happy about the move. My main concern, to be honest, was that I'm scared of the dark. If Daisy moved to another room, I'd have to deal with it again. Sure, we were crowded, but there were some alternatives. Why shouldn't Gratkins buy a bunk bed for my room? Or if she insisted on buying a second single bed, why couldn't Daisy and I move into a larger room? Both solutions seemed reasonable to me. But did Gratkins listen to reason?

"Crowding stifles the spirit," she stated firmly. "There's not much I can offer Daisy on my narrow income, but for once she'll have her own space."

"For once?" I echoed. "Does that mean you lived in a small house, Daisy? Or does it just mean you come from a large family?"

"We will return after these messages," said Daisy. What kind of answer was that?

"Quit talking TV," I said. "I wish *I* came from a large family. They'd be all boys except for me. I'd like an older brother."

"Oh, no, you wouldn't," Daisy mumbled through her mouthful of ground beef.

"Why? Do you have one?" I asked.

"No questions, Garet!" Gratkins gave me a warning look, which changed to a smile as she waved a furniture catalog in the air. "That warehouse on Mount Pleasant Street is having a sale. Every bed in the store is going for half price."

"Cool!" I said. "Daisy wants bunk beds. Don't you, Daisy?"

I lunged across the table to grab the catalog, and Daisy tried to grab it back again. I could tell she didn't want me in on the choosing, but I didn't know why yet.

"My birthday is only two months away," I reminded Gratkins. "How about bunk beds for *my* room?"

Gratkins said not to get impatient — she already had a present in mind for me, and it was something I'd wanted for a long time. This was good news; the only thing I'd wanted for a long time was a computer. So I quit nagging her and flipped through the catalog in search of bunk beds that might appeal to Daisy.

There were two different kinds on page 40: "Nautical" and "Nordic," but what caught my attention was the bed on page 41. It was made of dark wood polished to a rosy glow and had four tall posts at the corners. The posts were there to hold up a flowery, flouncy piece of cloth that matched the flowery, flouncy quilt. The minute I saw it, I wanted it. In fact I wanted it so badly that, for a while anyway, I forgot about the computer.

Someone, and I knew it wasn't Gratkins, had drawn a heart around that bed with a red marker. The bunk beds didn't even have the corner of the page turned down. I looked suspiciously at Daisy. Daisy blushed.

"It's high-impact romance at a low-impact price," she whispered.

I waited for Gratkins to gag, but I should have

known better. She actually thought Daisy was cute! "Let's hope they still have it in stock," she said. "I'll give them a call in the morning."

I was burning up inside, but I wasn't about to show it. "You're actually planning to sleep in that thing?" I asked Daisy, loading my voice with scorn. "You've got to be kidding! Who do you think you are, Scarlett O'Hara?"

"I'm Daisy Atkins." She was still whispering, but it was a stubborn whisper.

This made me burn even hotter. "Who says that's your name? Do you have any ID saying that's your name? I'm sick and tired of the Daisy Atkins mystery!"

I realize it was mean to pick on her just because Gratkins was buying her the bed I wanted for myself. It would have made more sense to be nice so she'd give me a chance to sleep in it once in a while. But I was jealous beyond reason.

"Half price means two for the price of one," I reminded Gratkins. "If you get one for Daisy, you can get one for me, too."

Gratkins said that if the bed weren't on sale, she couldn't buy it at all. She told Daisy not to get her hopes up because sale items went fast, so maybe it was too late. But it wasn't too late. Not only did the warehouse have one of those canopy beds left, it also turned out they were delivering in our neighborhood the same day we telephoned. So Daisy moved to a room down the hall, and I was alone in the dark again.

Now imagine me standing in the doorway of

Daisy's new room. Inside the room are just two things: Daisy and her bed. The bed looked great except for not having a quilt like the picture in the catalog. The quilt was not on sale. But if you think this spoiled Daisy's pleasure, you're wrong.

"How do you like it?" she asked.

"For something so cheap and tacky, it's not bad," I admitted. "Can I sleep in here tonight?"

Daisy pointed out that there wasn't a second bed.

"That's okay," I said. "I'll drag in the extra mattress."

Daisy said there wasn't room.

"What do you mean there isn't room?" I protested. "There's nothing *but* room. Even after you get some other furniture, there'll be plenty of room."

Daisy gave in. Why? Because she felt sorry for me. Why did she feel sorry for me? Because Gratkins decided to give me my birthday present ahead of time, and it was computer lessons. Not a computer. Just lessons.

When Daisy found out, she shook her head in a dazed kind of way. "I can't believe it!" she said. "That's not a present — that's a punishment. I guess you didn't play your cards right."

Daisy is a firm believer in playing your cards right. She thinks she does it and I don't. She's correct. I was mad at Gratkins for a while, but once I started the course, I changed my mind. Not only was it fun, I also learned to type fast, which is helpful for my autobiography. In fact, I'd better come right out and admit that those lessons were a really good present.

But Daisy couldn't know that back in August, so she let me sleep in her room.

Here's the hitch: I couldn't sleep. The sight of the canopy bed was more than I could stand. What was I doing on the floor while this intruder lay like a princess in a nest of frills? It was bad enough, the way Daisy had moved in and taken over. The bed was the final straw. Now I hated her.

"Why are you staring at me in that funny way?" Daisy asked after a while.

"It's not you," I said, cranking out a sardonic laugh. "It's your bed. From down here it sure looks silly."

Daisy's eyes grew all surprised and hurt. "It's not silly — it's romantic! I'm planning to have a bed just like this when I get married."

"Not me," I said. "When I get married, I'll have bunk beds. My husband and I are going to take turns sleeping on the upper bunk."

Daisy said that wasn't romantic. I said maybe not, but it sure would be fun. I told her she'd get bored with the flowery, flouncy canopy because it wasn't good for anything but looking at. If she had an upper bunk instead, she could look at it some nights and sleep on it others.

Daisy said she could sleep on the canopy, if she felt like it. "It doubles as a hammock," she informed me.

"It does not," I said.

"It does so," said Daisy.

"Prove it!" I said.

23

"I will someday," said Daisy. "Right now I don't feel like it."

"That's because you're chicken and you know you're wrong," I said.

"It is not," said Daisy.

"It is so," I said.

So she shinnied up a post to prove it, and there was this awful cracking, ripping noise. Daisy screamed and —

Chapter 3

— fell.

Which is how The Professional Author ends his chapters. The reason being, according to Mrs. Magorian, that he likes to leave you in suspense. Personally, I could do without too much suspense. Especially if the chapter is read aloud by a person who won't start the next one till tomorrow.

Daisy's accident was no big deal, except that accidents are more expensive at night because you have to go to the emergency room. Daisy got four stitches under her chin, and I got talked to. Not yelled at, just talked to. The talk went like this:

Gratkins: "I'm sorry this had to happen, Garet."

Garet: "Me, too. If only Daisy had listened to me and chosen the bunk beds!"

Gratkins: "Now, don't start that again, young lady. If you hadn't been there, the accident never would have occurred."

Garet:	"If Daisy hadn't been there, it never would have occurred, you mean."
Gratkins:	"Do I detect the presence of a green-eyed monster?"
Garet:	"Are you kidding? I think canopy beds are sleazy, and I wouldn't be Daisy for all the money in the world."
Gratkins:	[giving me this long, reproachful look] "I doubt there are many people who would want to be Daisy."
Garet:	[SILENCE. But this is what I was thinking: What's so bad about being Daisy? If I were Daisy, I'd be smart and pretty. If I were Daisy, Gratkins would spoil me. So the truth was that I'd give being Daisy a try for no money at all.]
Gratkins:	"It should be your life's purpose to see that Daisy feels loved and cherished, Garet."
Garet:	"You can't tell me what my life's purpose should be. I mean, it's *my* life, isn't it?"
Gratkins:	"Daisy is part of your life now."

By the time the doctor led Daisy out of the emergency room, guess who was crying? Not Daisy. Why should Daisy cry? She was getting the quilt that matched her canopy bed. Gratkins promised to buy it as a reward for being brave.

That's the end of the canopy bed story, so now I'm going to flash forward again. Flashing forward is trickier than flashing back. I know from the books I've read that there are two ways of doing it. One is just to quit the italic print and start the normal print again. The other is for the heroine to give a little shiver as she comes to her senses and remembers she's back in the present. I'm bored with both ways, so I've invented a third. It's called the Useful Gimmick Flash-Forward, and you guessed it: the gimmick is still shepherd's pie.

Imagine Daisy and Garet eating it (I should say, trying to eat it) yet again, but this time in September. Gratkins has already finished and is reading the paper. She's a little hard of hearing, so she doesn't notice that Garet is yet again begging Daisy to trade potatoes for meat.

"No, thanks," says Daisy.

Garet is in trouble. She searches desperately for ways to dispose of her meat. She says, "I wish we had a dog."

Daisy says, "Why don't you ask for one?"

Garet says, "Are you kidding? If it were that easy, I would have done it long ago."

Daisy says, "That's because you don't know the right way to ask."

"And I suppose you do?" says Garet.

Gratkins looks up from the paper. She glances suspiciously from Garet to Daisy and back to Garet again. She thought she heard the beginning of a quarrel. She decides she was wrong and returns to her horoscope.

"Let's see you do it, then," says Garet.

"No, thanks," says Daisy. "I don't want a dog."

Daisy gets on Garet's nerves. Garet loses her cool and calls Daisy a liar. Gratkins hears. She slaps her paper down on the table and asks Garet to apologize to her sister. Garet apologizes.

" 'Toward nightfall, Scorpios should opt for harmony,' " Gratkins reads aloud. "What's wrong with you girls?"

"Who says Daisy's a Scorpio?" I ask.

Gratkins says, "You ask too many questions."

"My eager young mind is hungry for knowledge," I tell her. "You wouldn't want to starve my eager young mind, would you?"

Meanwhile, Daisy opts for harmony. Smiling primly at me, she takes a tiny bite of meat and wipes her fork on her napkin before taking a tiny bite of potato. Over the past weeks she has become finickier than ever. Shepherd's pie is a real problem for her. You'd think Gratkins would get wise and eliminate it from the menu!

Daisy finally swallows her last bite of potato and carries her plate to the sink. But later she has the nerve to tell Garet that she, Daisy, can get pretty much anything she wants out of Gratkins.

"I got the canopy bed, didn't I?" she asks. "And then I got the matching quilt."

Garet laughs scornfully. "You're trying to tell me you fell and cut yourself on purpose just so you could get that quilt?"

"Of course not," says Daisy. "I just mean that once I cut myself, I made the best of it. It's easy — you can do it, too."

Of all the tricky little manipulators! "You mean if I break my arm or something, I'll get my own canopy bed?"

Daisy shrugs. "Whatever. But you don't have to break your arm. If you want a dog, for instance, all you have to do is sit in front of the TV all day and stare at the screen."

"What's the catch?" I ask.

Daisy says the catch is that you don't turn the TV on. I tell her she has to be joking. TV bores me anyway. Watching it with the power off would be the pits.

"It depends how much you want the dog," Daisy tells me with another shrug to show she couldn't care less. "If you really want the dog, you have to act disturbed. It would help if you stopped functioning at school, too."

"Stopped functioning?" I ask. "You mean stopped working? I don't need that kind of trouble."

"It depends how much you want the dog," she repeats in this cool, patient way. "If you want the dog, you have to come up with an emotional problem that having a dog would fix. I could be your problem, for instance."

I'm pretty sure she's making fun of me. She already is my problem, and she knows it.

"When there's a new baby in a family," Daisy explains, "wise parents will consider buying a pet for the older sibling. It's to keep the older sibling from feeling neglected."

I ask how she knows, and she says she learned it from a talk show. I should have guessed. Daisy has watched more TV in three months than I have in my entire life. She was heartbroken when school started and she couldn't watch the soaps anymore. Gratkins has to bring her up to date when she gets back. And this is supposed to be my twin?

"If you act disturbed long enough," she explains, "Gratkins will realize you're getting a poor self-image because she loves me more than she loves you."

"Why would she do that?" I ask.

"Because I'm smarter and prettier," says Daisy.

"Give me a break!" I say, because I'd sooner die than admit she's right.

Daisy says that's not the point. The point is what Gratkins thinks I think she thinks.

"It won't work," I say.

"It will so," says Daisy.

"*You* try it, then."

"I told you, I don't want a dog."

"Neither do I," I admit. "It's just that a dog would be useful for shepherd's pie. If I act disturbed, I'll do it for a laptop computer."

Daisy says a computer would be harder because it costs more than a dog and can't give you love and affection. "An emotional problem wouldn't be enough," she says thoughtfully. "You'd need a learning disability, too."

I tell her I don't have a learning disability, but she says it would be easy to fake one. I remind her that the kids at school with learning disabilities get extra tutoring, not laptop computers. She says the kids at school don't play their cards right. I say I wouldn't want to risk it.

"I bet you wouldn't either," I say.

"I would so," says Daisy.

"You would not," I say.

"How much do you want to bet?" she asks.

I say I'll bet a million dollars. She says I don't have a million dollars. I say I'll bet anything she likes, but she says she doesn't like anything I have so she won't bet after all.

"Chicken!" I say.

"I didn't say I wouldn't do it," she argues. "I just said I wouldn't bet. I want it to be a contest. If I win, I get to keep the computer."

"That's fine with me," I say. Because I'm dead sure she'll lose.

I should have known better. Daisy won, and the way she went about it was to spell words wrong. That is, she put the right letters in, but she put them in the wrong place. She did this in all her classes, not just English. At first the teachers thought she was being careless. They made her copy things over. But Daisy would stare at the word with a disabled expression on her face and copy it wrong again. Then she would cry.

She got extra tutoring, of course. But the tutor had a remedial program on one of the Whetstone Academy computers. Whenever Daisy used the computer, she spelled right. Toward the end of October, the tutor told Gratkins that Daisy had a hand-eye coordination problem. It was really frustrating for Daisy, the tutor explained, to be unable to express all the creative thoughts she had in her eager young mind. In the long run, it would undermine her self-image. In the short run, she should be encouraged to do her homework on her own personal laptop computer.

Which she got for my thirteenth birthday. What I got was a dog. I didn't expect to get anything, since Gratkins is always broke and she had already given me computer lessons. So why the dog? Because Daisy told Gratkins it was what I wanted most in the whole world. And why did Daisy get the computer on my birthday? Because Gratkins decided it should be Daisy's birthday, too.

I thought this was a terrible idea. Gratkins and I happen to have been born on the same day. On October 29 we always had a special celebration, just for the two of us. I wasn't about to share. "Daisy has her own room," I reasoned. "Why can't she have her own birthday, too?"

"Because people think you're twins," was the obvious answer.

I appealed to Daisy. "You must have a real birthday. When is it?"

"October twenty-ninth," she said stubbornly.

"Well, don't expect any present from me," I told her. Then I asked Gratkins what *she* wanted for her birthday. She answered that the nicest present I could give her would be to live in harmony with my new sister.

Well, I tried. And I'm still trying, which brings me gracefully back to the present. It took me a long time to write this flashback, so several days have passed since I started it. But in case you're wondering, we did indeed have shepherd's road-kill pie for lunch.

Mrs. Magorian says I've had ample time to write

about my childhood. She says I should move out of my past and into my future. Whoever heard of an autobiography of someone's future? The only sure thing about my future is shepherd's pie.

Footnote: Mrs. Magorian says every well-documented autobiography has footnotes. They're in case The Intelligent Reader seeks additional information. I'm sure you want to know what I named my dog, but if you're really intelligent, you already guessed that I named him Laptop. He likes shepherd's pie.

Footnote #2: The computer wasn't all Daisy got. It didn't take long for her to convince Gratkins that it was useless without a printer, for instance. And that she needed the StudyCenter Desk from Computer Shack to put the printer and computer on. And the OrthoPedant BackSaver Chair. And the NonGlare EyeSaver Lamp. If Daisy said she couldn't do her homework unless she was wearing a 24-karat gold WristSaver Bracelet, you can bet your life she'd get that, too. But even greed has its limits.

Chapter 4

Surprise, surprise! Daisy's learning disability cleared up fast. Even writing cursive, she never mixes up her letters anymore. Everybody (meaning Gratkins and the teachers) said it was thanks to the computer. But somebody (meaning me) happens to know the truth.

Daisy couldn't care less about computers. She only uses her laptop to play a home education game called *Zappo!* It's supposed to teach you touch-typing, spelling, and grammar all in one program where you get to be a character called Mr. SpelGud. If you play it right, Mr. SpelGud stores up punctuation marks as ammunition and zaps the enemy. Your mistakes are the enemy. This game is no fun unless you cheat. The way to cheat is to ignore the touch-typing part and play with two fingers. Daisy cheats.

I hardly ever use the laptop either, for two simple reasons:

1. Daisy hardly ever lets me, and
2. I'm too busy with the other Laptop: the furry

34

four-legged one. He's better company than the rest of my so-called family these days.

When I came back from walking Laptop yesterday morning, I went to check whether Daisy was ready for school. Getting ready takes forever now that she's a media freak. Her ambition is to dress like anchorwomen on TV, but her outfits are put together from things she finds in the attic. The results are not what your typical Academy girl wears. Not what your typical anchorwoman wears either.

Most days Daisy is late, and most days I don't mind. But yesterday morning I did happen to mind because it had been nearly a week since I worked on my autobiography. The reason is that last Monday the fourth-graders were let loose in the computer room for LAP, which stands for Language Awareness Program. The computers spent the next two days in intensive care. Mrs. Magorian got permission for 7-B to spend all of yesterday making up for the time lost on our SWAP projects. I didn't want to miss a single minute.

"What's going on in there?" I yelled, banging on Daisy's door. "Gratkins is already out in the car."

When Daisy didn't answer, I went in. And I couldn't believe what she was doing. Usually if Daisy is late, it's because she's in tears, trying on every outfit in her closet. This time she was in tears, all right, but it was over *Zappo!*

"What's the matter?" I asked.

I leaned over her shoulder and watched Mr. SpelGud zap a dangling participle with an asterisk. While the zapping took place, the computer beeped

35

its shrill computer tune and Daisy made a repulsive snuffling noise through her nose.

"You're winning, aren't you?" I asked. "Not that it really counts unless you use all your fingers."

Daisy was using two. She tapped the keys with one forefinger whose nail glowed from a triple coat of hot pink polish and one forefinger whose nail was bitten to the quick. The other fingers were clenched into a tight fist.

"How come you're ready so early?" I asked.

Not only was she ready, she looked as if she had put more time than usual into getting that way. She had French-braided her hair, a thing she never does on weekdays because it takes so long. She was wearing rhinestone earrings and a matching pin in the shape of a poodle. I had seen the pin and earrings in the attic but never dreamed of wearing them. The only jewelry I wear is the key to my room on a string around my neck. I've taken to doing that in case I need privacy, now that Daisy has moved in.

"Is this National Suck-Up-to-Your-Teacher Day or something?" I asked.

Because believe it or not, she was also wearing pantyhose, plus the party shoes she had on when she slid out of the laundry chute. The rest of her was less formal: a jeans skirt (you're not allowed to wear jeans pants at Whetstone), a tank top, and the vest from my great-grandfather's wedding suit.

"You look great," I said untruthfully. "Can we go now?"

Daisy fished a damp wad of Kleenex out of her pocket and blew her nose. While she was blowing, a runaway sentence appeared on the screen and zapped Mr. SpelGud. He shrank rapidly. Then he died and the game was over. I turned it off.

"You're going to make me late," I said.

Daisy's nose made that repulsive noise again. Suddenly I wished I hadn't eaten breakfast. "What's the matter, didn't you get your homework done on time?"

Her shoulders heaved as she sobbed out her answer: "I'm homesick!"

For three months, Daisy had refused to breathe a word about her home. Was she finally going to open up? Not wanting her to see how curious I was, I began to stroll casually around the room, looking at all her things.

You may wonder how Daisy collected so many things in the short time she lived with us. The answer is she brought them down from the attic. Not just clothes: also a gold-framed mirror that was murky with age, some leather-bound books with illustrations, and a bunch of toys, including a Noah's ark with wooden animals inside. Mind you, none of this stuff was valuable, or it would have been sold long ago. The mirror was cracked, and the books were missing pages. They were pretty cool all the same, and I told Gratkins she should make Daisy share. Gratkins said I was free to forage in the attic for myself, but I don't have Daisy's greedy eye for treasure.

Now, when I said Daisy was finicky about food, it's nothing to the way she is about her room. I keep my own things mainly on the floor so I know where to find them. Not Daisy. She doesn't even keep her shoes on the floor. Instead she lines them up on a shelf in her closet. In pairs, as if it would break their little hearts to be apart. And that's not all. Her books are arranged by color. And her Noah's ark animals are lined up according to height, pointing in the same direction. All the things on her desk have to point in the same direction, too. Even the paper clips. If they don't, she can't get to sleep.

"I hardly slept at all last night," said Daisy.

I was about to ask whether a paper clip had stepped out of line, but she looked so upset that I resisted the temptation. "Why not?" I asked instead.

"It's noisy here," she said.

Noisy? Our big empty house? With Laptop prowling around at night, even the mice have moved away.

"I don't mean inside," she explained, reading my mind. "Inside it's quiet as a tomb. Sometimes the quiet wakes me up at night, and I lie there wondering where everybody is."

"Now, wait just a minute!" I protested. "You can't have it both ways. Either it's too quiet to sleep or it's too noisy to sleep, but not both at once."

Her voice rose into a pathetic, wobbly wail. "You don't understand. It's so different!"

Now was my chance. "You mean, from where you use to live? What's it like where you use to live?"

A faraway look came into Daisy's eyes. She took a deep breath and calmed down a little as she spoke. "Different, that's all. Noisier inside, with people in every room. And house noises. I'm not sure what: maybe hot water pipes. It was warmer then. You and Gratkins don't keep this place warm enough."

"Maybe you'd like to pay the oil bill?"

She ignored my sarcasm. "I can't. Anyway, I still like it here, even if it's cold. It's outdoors that bothers me, with all those cars circling around the house."

I began to worry. Was Daisy losing her mind? "Stop exaggerating. You make it sound like a merry-go-round."

"Oh, you know what I mean," she said. "This place has streets all around it. There's just a scrap of lawn in front and back, and hardly any trees, and the headlights come in my window all night long."

"Did you use to live in the country?" I asked.

She sighed. "Not exactly. But there was a lot more land, and the neighbors were farther away, and there weren't so many roads or cars."

"You lived in the country." I was beginning to lose patience with her. "Why don't you go back there, if you're homesick?"

Daisy stared at me for a long time. Her face had a funny expression: half wanting to say more, but half suspicious. She remained silent.

I moved toward the door. "Could we please leave for school? It's time to go."

Daisy didn't budge. "I got up while it was still dark," she informed me. "I didn't know what to do, so I dressed up extra nice. Then I still didn't know what to do, so I played *Zappo!*"

I shrugged. "What's wrong with that?"

"It doesn't work is what's wrong." Daisy gave her desk a kick, making the computer beep its tune once more, even though I had turned it off. She blew her nose again.

It was getting awfully red. Her nose, not the

computer. Her eyes were red, too, and oddly smudgy. She must have put on makeup, which is against the rules at Whetstone. There was no way she'd leave home if she knew how bad it looked. My chances of getting to school on time were growing slimmer. If I wanted to spend the day writing my autobiography, I'd have to keep her away from the mirror.

"It does so work," I told her. "I saw it working. You're getting pretty good at it, too."

This was a lie. Daisy is a real klutz at computers. I know she's smart, so it must be she's scared of them. As I said, she only uses her laptop to play *Zappo!* But even at *Zappo!* she's no good. She's no good at any kind of video game. When we go to the arcades she forgets to put the quarter in, and she can't figure out why she never wins.

Daisy smiled. She reacts fast to flattery.

"The game works fine," she admitted. "It's just the date that's broken, when you turn the computer on."

"Don't take it personally," I advised her. "People break dates all the time."

I thought this was pretty funny, but Daisy cried harder than ever. "It says 1943! It got November 11 right, but even though I kept pushing the delete key and typing it over again, it wouldn't say 1993. And I swear I'm not doing it on purpose."

It was like a bad joke. Whoever heard of a learning-disabled computer? Come to think of it, it was a *good* joke on Daisy. Except it was making me late.

Daisy's laptop works differently from the school computers, so I'd better explain. When you turn the school computers on, they flash the date at you. But with Daisy's laptop, you have to type it in before entering a program. This isn't as much of a pain as it sounds because if you don't know the date, you can make one up and the computer will accept it. One thing is certain: it won't tell you you're fifty years off.

"I'll try it when we get back this afternoon," I said. "You must be doing something wrong."

She looked more hopeful, so I thought maybe I could sweet-talk her out to the car. Unfortunately, Gratkins chose that moment to lean on the horn. Daisy hurried to her mirror. This meant my chances of getting to school on time were nonexistent, so I gave the laptop my full attention. First I unplugged it and plugged it in again. Then I checked the place where the cord goes into the machine. Everything seemed okay. I switched on the power and waited for the screen to light up.

"Let's see the manual again," I said. Not that I needed it, but I wanted to be sure I got everything right.

Any normal person would keep the manual handy to the computer, but not Daisy. The manual is yellow, so it has to go with the yellow books on the shelf, right? The other yellow books are Nancy Drews, but Daisy has a logic of her own.

"Let's see now," I murmured, reading the instructions aloud. " 'After completion of the boot procedure, the computer screen will flash a system prompt requesting current date. Before accessing any peripherals —' "

"What's a peripheral?" Daisy asked. "How do you access one, anyway? I never understood that part."

"Never mind," I said. "The point is the date. Here's what we want: 'Type current date in Arabic numerals, following window prompts. The screen will respond showing day of week.' Big deal! I never forget the day of the week. It's the day of the month I lose track of. Why can't it just tell you, like the school computers?"

"Because it's more high-tech," said Daisy.

Taking my time, I typed "11/11/93." Then I punched "Enter." The computer beeped a couple of times before the screen came up with "Thurs., Nov. 11, 1993."

"You were tired," I told Daisy. "You said yourself you hardly slept at all. And digital fours are easy to confuse with nines."

I didn't believe this for a minute. Daisy was just being klutzy again. But I was nice enough to spare her feelings, so it didn't seem fair for her turn on me.

"You think I'm stupid!" she said, practically hissing, she was so mad. "Just because you took lessons and I didn't. Well, I know how to work my own computer, and I know there's something wrong with it. Watch this!"

She pushed me out of the way and started the whole procedure over again. She was mad all right, but she was careful. I watched her every step of the way, and there wasn't the slightest doubt that she typed "93," not "43." But "43" is what appeared on the screen.

"See what I mean?" Daisy wailed. "It's wrong by half a century!"

I have to admit, it really was bizarre. I made her try a second time, just to make sure, but it happened again. Then I punched in the date myself and it came out right.

"I know what," I said. "I'll type 11/11/43 and see what happens."

What happened was that the computer took offense. It beeped indignantly for thirty seconds before flashing a message at me. The message said, "Device timeout. Illegal parameter. Abort? Delete? Ignore?"

I wasn't anxious for it to do any of those things to me, so I turned it off.

That's when Gratkins walked in. She was jingling her car keys impatiently, but after one look at Daisy's face, she dropped the keys and said, "Honey! What's wrong?"

I took off my jacket and went to the kitchen for a second breakfast. We were already half an hour late.

It is totally untrue that I created this incident out of my "singularly convoluted imagination" (Mrs. Magorian's exact words) in order to come up with an excuse for missing school yesterday. I *wanted* to go to school yesterday. I didn't have a red nose, did I? I wasn't wearing makeup, was I? I wasn't even wearing hot pink nail polish. I wouldn't be caught dead with it.

The one and only thing on my mind that morning was my autobiography. I told Gratkins there was no reason why I shouldn't go to school alone. She and Daisy could stay home and watch the soaps together.

I pleaded. And I begged. But I guess I didn't play my cards right, because her answer was always no.

What we did instead was go on a family picnic "to support Daisy during this time of stress" (Gratkins's exact words). I admit that once I knew there was no hope of school, I looked forward to the picnic. I expected Daisy to break down and explain a few things. I bet The Intelligent Reader expects it, too. "It's about time!" you're saying to yourself. "Garet is finally going to get some answers."

Answers? Garet? Dream on! This is the way our conversation went:

Garet: "So start talking, Daisy. Where's this place in the country you're so homesick for? Why did you run away from it? Who are you, anyway?"

Gratkins: "You ask too many questions."

Daisy not only refused to talk; she also refused to eat. This is because Gratkins made peanut butter and jelly sandwiches. She forgot that Daisy gags if you mix the two together.

The only good news is that Daisy made such a fuss about the broken date that Gratkins took her laptop back to Computer Shack to be overhauled. It serves Daisy right. Now she can't even play *Zappo!*

Mrs. Magorian says this ought to be called "The Daisy Atkins Story." I hate it when Mrs. Magorian tries to be funny. She says I've hardly started on my own life yet. Boy, is that ever true! But what makes her think I have one?

Chapter 5

Today is Sunday. No, they haven't started making us go to school on weekends. Not yet. And no, Daisy didn't give in and lend me her computer. She couldn't if she wanted to because it's still in the shop. So how am I writing this? By hand, that's how. On a pad of paper, with a pencil. It feels peculiar!

The reason is that I don't want to forget two conversations I had this morning: one with Gratkins and one with Daisy. I figure this way I can copy them into the Whetstone computer tomorrow morning without wasting my time praying for total recall.

This morning it snowed. It was already snowing when I woke up, and it kept on snowing for an hour. We got two inches. It was the first snow of the season, so it was kind of exciting. The leaves have mostly fallen off their branches. There are just a few yellow ones left, plus the brown ones on the oak trees, which stay longest of all. When the snow landed on them, it looked like powdered sugar sprinkled on a mixture of bran flakes and cornflakes. I was sitting up in bed and looking out the window, wondering if Daisy would gag over a mixture of bran flakes and corn-flakes, when in walked Daisy herself. Without knock-ing.

"Next time, knock," I said.

"Good morning," said Daisy.

I stared at her. What was she trying to do, start the day by picking a fight?

"Didn't you hear me?" I asked.

Daisy shrugged. "Next time, I'll knock. Want to take Laptop for a walk?"

I stared even harder. She was dressed for walking, all right. Daisy has an outfit planned for each thing she does or might be asked to do. Skateboarding, for instance. Daisy doesn't know how to skateboard and doesn't want to learn. If she changed her mind, how-ever, she plans to wear a pale pink ballet tutu over pink silk tights with her navy cable-knit on top. She has a little notebook with lists of what she'd wear for every occasion: going to the dentist, appearing on a TV talk show, riding a camel. Honest to God, Daisy planned an outfit for riding a camel!

The walking outfit consists of her baby blue Nikes, designer jeans, a purple velvet jacket that she found in the attic, and a feather boa. This morning she wore the boa pulled across her forehead and trail-ing down behind.

"What's that for?" I asked.

She said it was a sweatband. This really cracked me up. Daisy is the last person in the world to need a sweatband. Why? Because she doesn't sweat. She doesn't even like walking unless it's the only way to get where she needs to go.

"Forget it," I told her. "I don't want to take Laptop for a walk, and you don't either."

"I do so," she said.

"You do not," I said.

"Why not?" she asked.

"Because I know you, and it's just not your style," I told her.

Daisy looked at me for a while with a weird, goofy expression on her face.

"Do you really know me?" she asked finally.

"Of course I do."

"Would you know me tomorrow?"

"What do you mean? Of course I would."

"How about next week? How about next year?"

I groaned. "Daisy, what are you getting at?"

"Knock, knock!" said Daisy.

I fell for it. "Who's there?"

"See what I mean?"

Smiling the tight kind of smile where you practically swallow your lips, Daisy walked out the door.

I locked my door behind me before I went down to breakfast. Gratkins saw me do it, and asked why.

"Crowding stifles the spirit, remember?" I answered, quoting her own words. "When Daisy barges in without knocking, my spirit gets an asthma attack."

Gratkins said that people who saw the key around my neck would take me for a latchkey child and think she neglected me. I told her I'd wear it inside my shirt if she'd rather, but it was my personal right to lock

47

Daisy out of my room.

She gave me a sour look. "You'd lock Daisy out of your life if you could get away with it. I know you!"

Did she really? After breakfast, I said, and I tried Daisy's joke on her. She was prepared for it, though. When I got to the "Knock, knock!" part, she just said, "Why, it's Garet!"

"Oh," I said. "Did Daisy already try it on you?"

Instead of answering, she sighed. "It's an interesting joke. I wonder how well we actually do know each other."

It seemed like the perfect opportunity for a good heart-to-heart about Daisy.

"I know you hate me to ask questions," I said for starters. "All the same, since I'm letting her be my twin, don't I have a right to know where she came from?"

Gratkins had been cleaning the kitchen sink. This is one of the few jobs she won't let me or Daisy do, because she enjoys it so much. Our kitchen sink belongs in a museum. The flat part is made of marble, and it's perched on a jungle gym of copper pipes. Gratkins must be the only grandmother in the world with the energy to clean it.

"Want help?" I offered as usual.

"No, thanks," she answered as usual. "I'm having too much fun."

Fun! It looks like punishment to me. She doesn't even use normal household products. Instead she scours it with an old toothbrush and then polishes it with an old sock. The result is magnificent, but in my opinion it's wasted on a sink. Gratkins was at the pol-

48

ishing stage when I asked her my question about Daisy. I could tell she was upset, because she picked up the toothbrush and started scouring all over again.

"Don't I have a right to know where she came from?" I repeated.

Gratkins frowned into the sink. "Daisy came down the laundry chute, if your story is correct."

"Oh, come on!" I protested. "You know perfectly well what I mean. Where did she come from before that?"

Gratkins shrugged. Then she turned the hot water on full blast, rinsed out the sink, and set to work with the sock again. "If you have nothing better to do, you might take a sponge and wipe the fingerprints off the pantry cupboard," she said. "Someone's been poking around in there with dirty hands."

I sprinkled some cleanser on a sponge and began to scrub.

"Don't wipe off the family yardstick!" she warned me.

The family yardstick consists of a series of lines and dates on the pantry cupboard door. Gratkins and her eight brothers and sisters used to get measured there from year to year, to mark how they grew. My heights are on there, too, from when I came to live with Gratkins right up to now.

"I'll be careful," I promised. "If Daisy is my sister, why isn't she on here, too?"

It was just a casual remark, but Gratkins took it the wrong way. "Questions, questions! When are you going to stop asking so many questions?"

"When I get some honest answers," I said crossly.

"If you know something about Daisy, it isn't fair not to tell. And you *must* know something about her. Otherwise why would you be spoiling her the way you do?"

That got her attention. Gratkins put down the sock and stared at me. "Spoiling her, Garet? How do you mean?"

I had meant to keep cool, but this was too much for me. I'm afraid I started whining like a four-year-old. I whined about Daisy's new room and all the furniture in it, with special emphasis on the canopy bed. I whined about the Noah's ark. And you can imagine what I sounded like by the time I got to the laptop computer.

Gratkins was so surprised that she started breathing in little gasps. "Honey, I had no idea you felt this way. Not an inkling!"

I was so close to tears by now that I talked extra fast, while I could still talk at all. "I want to know why she's your favorite," I said. "It's because she's prettier and smarter, isn't it? Don't lie to me!"

Gratkins did something unexpected: she laughed. And as soon as she started laughing, I broke down and cried.

"I'm sorry, honey," Gratkins said, and she hugged me with wet, soapy arms that smelled of drains and detergent. "I know it doesn't seem funny to you, but I can tell you one thing. Daisy isn't prettier or smarter than you. You're exactly as smart and pretty as each other, and you always will be."

"Yeah, sure!" I pulled away from her, feeling mistrustful and embarrassed. "If you're going to start telling things, I'd rather you told me where she comes from."

After all that fuss, can you guess what Gratkins answered? She looked me straight in the eye and said, "Daisy came down the laundry chute."

Chapter 6

I'm in hot water, and all because of a mood.

Not the usual kind of mood, mind you, such as when I get out the wrong side of my non-bunk, non-canopy bed. At Whetstone Academy for Girls they couldn't care less about that kind of mood as long as you keep it to yourself. No, I'm talking about the mood of my autobiography.

"The Professional Author," Mrs. Magorian told us on Wednesday, "establishes the mood of a piece on page one. Are you girls aware of the mood you have set in your autobiographies?"

We all looked at each other. We all scrunched down in our seats. We all kept our mouths shut.

"Is it upbeat?" Mrs. Magorian asked. "Is it melancholy? Is it pensive or humorous? Have you created an aura of romance or mystery?"

Ardeth Shaeffer raised her hand, so Mrs. Magorian pounced on her and asked which. But it turned out that Ardeth just wanted permission to go to the girls' room.

I can always tell when there's extra homework coming on. The teachers start breathing faster, to begin with. Then they get this crazed expression on their faces. Mrs. Magorian was doing both things now. It struck me that if one of us didn't come up with a mood pretty soon, we'd have to spend an hour that evening trying to invent one. I raised my hand before I even knew what I was going to say.

"I'm not too sure about my own mood," I said, looking desperately around at the other girls in 7-B. "I know what Priscilla Perry's is, though."

Priscilla gave me a dirty look, but I ignored it. She didn't need extra homework either, so I figured she should be grateful. "It's equestrian," I said.

I was really proud of coming up with this word, but Mrs. Magorian just looked pained. "Equestrian, Garet? Kindly explain yourself."

I did. *Equestrian* means having to do with horses. Priscilla Perry is the horsiest person I know. Horsier than horses, even. Of course I didn't say how she looks like a horse and laughs like a horse. I didn't want to hurt her feelings. Besides, everyone in 7-B already knows it. But I passed a note down the row saying that if Priscilla's autobiography ever got published and someone wanted to buy it, unless that someone looked carefully at the photo on the dust jacket, they'd think the author was a horse.

Unfortunately, Mrs. Magorian intercepted the note. It wasn't signed, so she glared at us all except Priscilla and said, "Girls, I'm afraid some of you aren't taking this assignment seriously. Perhaps it would help if you printed out your diskettes."

At first I was glad. I'd been dying to see what my autobiography looked like in real book print, on paper. But when I found out it was because Mrs. Magorian wanted to take our autobiographies home and read them, I smelled trouble.

"I'm nowhere near finished!" I objected.

Mrs. Magorian said, "Naturally, Garet. The story of your life will finish only in the grave."

She's wrong. *Dead* wrong. Because I plan to come back and haunt her. She not only humiliated me in class the next day, she also put me through a parent-teacher conference that was nearly the undoing of my family, such as it is.

Things started out okay. Mrs. Magorian beamed at us when we all trooped into English class. She had a stack of manila folders on her desk, and I could see right away they were our autobiographies.

"Girls, I have many, many moods here before me," she announced. "I have sad moods, merry moods! Some of you are earnest, some are sentimental, and some are passionate!"

We all looked around to see who was passionate, but whoever it was wanted to keep it a secret.

"One thing is obvious," Mrs. Magorian continued. "That's the fact that you are all good writers."

I could hear an enormous sigh of relief. I was part of it until Mrs. Magorian handed back every folder but one and said, "Garet Atkins, would you like to have a word with me after class, please?"

Of all the things I'd like to do after English class, having a word with Mrs. Magorian is last on my list.

I would rather eat a Whetstone Academy cafeteria lunch composed entirely of crushed cat, for instance. But I wasn't given a choice. Not even the choice of conveniently forgetting I was supposed to stay, because Mrs. Magorian stood by the door as we filed out.

"Just a moment, Garet," she said, grabbing my arm. "Don't worry, I won't make you late for Health and Hygiene. Not that you seem to mind on other occasions."

I pretended to ignore her sarcastic tone and said, "Thank you, Mrs. Magorian."

Leading me back to her desk, she picked up my folder. I noticed, as she opened it and leafed through the pages, that it looked different from when I handed it in.

Riddle: What's black and white and red all over?
Answer: Garet Atkins's autobiography.

From what I could see, every page of my first five chapters had been marked up by Mrs. Magorian's red pencil. My heart thumped as I waited to hear what she would say. Her first comment was that my autobiography was long. I took this as a compliment.

"I come in and work on it during recess," I told her proudly. This happens to be true, but I should have kept my mouth shut because she asked who gave me permission.

"I didn't think you had to have permission to work on school assignments," I said.

She gave me a lecture on how the computers are Whetstone Academy property and I shouldn't just borrow one as if it were a soccer ball. I said I hadn't moved it, not one inch, and she said I knew perfectly well what she meant. Besides, there was such a thing as carrying a school assignment too far.

"More than fifty pages!" she added, sighing her martyred teacher sigh. "I made a few comments in the margins with my red pencil. I'd like you to take time to read them and make adjustments if you see fit."

I took the folder from her, but I couldn't take my eyes off her face. I felt both scared and fascinated, which I guess is how a mouse feels when it meets a snake.

"What if I don't see fit?"

This was a reasonable question in my opinion, so I don't see why she got upset. Her nose twitched as she told me that even The Professional Author has room for improvement, and as for me — I have far, far to go!

"Some of the grammar may be wrong," I admitted.

She shook her head. "Your grammar tends to be on the informal side, but it has its charm. No, it's your mood that troubles me."

"What's wrong with my mood?" I asked.

"It's callous," said Mrs. Magorian. "Your attitude toward your sister's learning disability, for example — amusing, but insensitive. Where, in these pages, are you really thinking about Daisy?"

I gasped. How inconsistent can a person get?

"Wait a minute! You told me there was too much about Daisy in here. You said it should be called 'The Daisy Atkins Story.' "

She sighed again. "True. But you've put in facts, not feelings. I'd understand if your preoccupation with Daisy came from genuine concern. But I'm afraid it looks more like ghoulish curiosity. And in places, you abandon fact altogether and spill over into fiction."

"Where?" I demanded. "Show me."

Mrs. Magorian frowned. "You know perfectly well what I mean, Garet. I'm speaking of your denial that Daisy is your sister. To say nothing of the myth you invented in which she appears out of a laundry chute."

"That's no myth," I informed her. "It happened."

Mrs. Magorian told me not to be cute. She said I was past the age of believing babies came from cabbage plants. When I reminded her that Daisy had been going on thirteen at the time, she said not to be impertinent. I could see we weren't getting anywhere. Food smells began drifting into the classroom, and during one silence, my stomach growled.

"Do you intend to continue this foolishness in the face of common sense and logic?" Mrs. Magorian asked.

I said yes, I did. "And it's not foolishness," I added. "It's the honest-to-God truth. Gratkins says so twice in chapter five. Didn't you read that part?"

She just stared at me with a cold look on her face, so I asked, "Are you calling Gratkins a liar?"

That question led me straight to the headmistress's office. The headmistress was out to lunch, thank goodness, but Mrs. Magorian made me sit there while she got the files for me and Daisy and looked up our telephone number.

"I would have told you if you'd asked me for it," I said when I saw her dialing. "I'm not a liar either."

Gratkins was at home. I didn't know if I was sorry or glad when she agreed to come over for a conference. But I had no say in the matter, or in the matter of getting Daisy up from the cafeteria to join us.

By now I was hungry. The food smells were driving me out of my mind, which is maybe why I lost my temper. Ordinarily I know better than to sass a teacher, but I'm afraid I called Mrs. Magorian a five-letter word and asked what business it was of hers how Daisy came into our family. Her answer nearly made me faint. It seems that while she was looking through the files for our phone number, she also looked for the copy of Daisy's birth certificate that Gratkins was supposed to give the school. There wasn't one.

"So what?" I asked weakly. "Do you think it means she wasn't born, or something?"

"Don't be rude, Garet," said Mrs. Magorian. "I'm sure it's merely an oversight on the part of your grandmother, who has enough on her hands, raising two teenage girls. But you see, if Daisy truly turned up out of nowhere, as you pretend, it would be a matter for the police."

The police? Suddenly I felt sick. What if the police found out where Daisy came from, and took her back there? She's a pain in the neck, but that doesn't mean I wish she'd go home. Or to a foster home, if she doesn't have a real one. Plus I don't want my grandmother in jail. Keeping a child who doesn't belong to you may be the same as kidnapping, which is a criminal offense. When Gratkins arrived and gave me an inquiring look, I nearly cried.

The amazing thing about that conference is the way Daisy backed me up. She told me afterward that she was just playing her cards right. Personally, I think it was ESP. The minute she walked into the office, she sensed there was trouble, and she took sides. My side.

"Hi, Garet!" she said. "Why weren't you at lunch?"

"You're about to find out," I said. "What *was* lunch?"

"Road kill," she answered sweetly, and sat down.

There was a pause while Mrs. Magorian shot Daisy a suspicious glance. Daisy smiled back, polite and innocent.

"What seems to be the problem?" Gratkins asked.

I'm not going to waste time telling how Mrs. Magorian said that relations between me and Daisy seemed a little strained and that the role of the school was to provide us with the name of a good family therapist. During this part we all squirmed in our chairs. I'll just pass on to the part about Daisy's birth certificate.

Mrs. Magorian is a lot different with parents than she is with us kids. It would have been funny if I hadn't been so scared. She put on this sympathetic voice as she explained to Gratkins about our autobiographies. Then she described my "myth" about the laundry chute. She had my folder with her and read some parts out of it.

"I know better than to take it seriously, of course," she said. And she was downright apologetic as she asked Gratkins for a copy of Daisy's birth certificate.

I watched Gratkins during all this. She seemed more worried than I'd ever seen her before. At the end of Mrs. Magorian's little speech, she turned to look at me. All she said was, "Garet!" Only she said it so reproachfully that my name turned into a groan.

"I thought it was like a diary," I explained. "I never thought anyone would be snoopy enough to read it."

I meant this to embarrass Mrs. Magorian, but she just said, "It was a class assignment, Mrs. Atkins. I suggest you take Garet's folder home with you and glance through it. Perhaps it will shed some light on the matter."

I squirmed some more. Gratkins squirmed, too. But what did Daisy do? Daisy opened her eyes really wide and said, "My goodness, I feel terrible! I'm the one who made Garet tell that story about me."

Mrs. Magorian looked surprised and relieved. Gratkins just looked surprised. As for me, I kept my mouth shut. I figured I'd better hear what Daisy had to say before I got us into any more trouble.

"Gratkins gave me the birth certificate to bring to school," Daisy went on. "But I hid it instead."

I stared at her. What birth certificate? Could Daisy

have had one in her pocket when she came down the laundry chute? Why would she hide it? None of this made sense!

Mrs. Magorian stared, too. For once she seemed at a loss for words. "Well?" she prompted after a long silence.

Daisy lowered her eyes until her lashes brushed against her cheeks. It looked fake, but very becoming. "There's something about me that I don't like people to know. Something embarrassing."

Boy, is Daisy smart! If she thought for a million years, she couldn't have come up with a better conversation stopper. Mrs. Magorian actually blushed. She must have a dirty mind. Her voice was pure syrup as she told me that anything I wrote in my autobiography would be confidential. In fact, she would make an exception and let me finish it before showing it to anyone at all, herself included.

"On condition that you're truthful, dear," she said.

Then she told Gratkins that a copy of Daisy's birth certificate had to be on file by the beginning of next week, although she promised it would be confidential, too. She said Daisy should bring it straight to her. That way Mrs. Magorian would file it so not even the school secretary would get to see it. Gratkins agreed and said the things parents always say when they're in a hurry to get out of teacher conferences. She still seemed worried.

Mrs. Magorian finally glanced at her watch. "I'm glad we've been able to clear up this little misunderstanding," she said cheerily. "That's what Whetstone

Academy is for, isn't it, girls? And I hope we all feel comfortable with the results."

Gratkins stood up, looking dazed. As she moved toward the door, she tried to stuff one of the files into her handbag, which is big, but not that big. I giggled, but Mrs. Magorian didn't think it was funny at all.

"No, no, Mrs. Atkins!" she cried, bounding after her. "That's Garet's official file, and it stays right here. It's her *folder* that I asked you to look through."

Gratkins pulled the file out of her bag again, scattering papers everywhere. Then she said that she wasn't interested in reading my autobiography until it was finished. This was a relief to me, but it annoyed Mrs. Magorian, who said that perhaps the three of us should just go home for the rest of the day.

I was grateful. I could hardly wait to see Daisy's birth certificate, but Gratkins had other ideas. She told us that the session at Whetstone had been stressful and that we should gather our forces by going for ice cream.

I wasn't too enthusiastic about this idea. It takes a lot of will power to be slim and mature looking, and I have more will power when I'm not looking at a menu than when I am. But Daisy and Gratkins never worry about their weight, so we drove to an ice cream parlor.

"I'll have a single scoop of frozen yogurt, no cone," I said virtuously.

"I'll have a banana split with fudge sauce on the side," Daisy said. "And I'd like an extra plate."

Did this mean she'd share with me? I decided to

give in if she asked. After all, I'd skipped lunch. But it turned out that the extra plate was to keep things separate. And believe me, separating a banana split takes forever.

"Give me a break, Daisy!" I said.

Gratkins said, "Leave your sister alone."

First Daisy put the cherry on the other plate. Then she scooped off the nuts and put them in a tidy little heap about an inch away from the cherry. She did the same thing for the whipped cream. After which she carefully extracted the banana and wiped it off with her napkin. All that was left on the first plate was the ice cream.

"Satisfied?" I asked.

Daisy said, "Not yet."

She still had to separate the scoop of vanilla from the scoop of chocolate and scrape off the side of each scoop that had rubbed against the other scoop. By the time she was ready to eat, Gratkins had finished her banana split. The waiter was standing with the check, his eyes bulging.

"You know what, Daisy?" I said. "You're a lunatic."

Gratkins got really mad. At me, not Daisy. She said something about tolerance for other people's habits and told me I'd made enough trouble for one day.

"Who's making trouble?" I asked. "I'm waiting patiently, aren't I? So is the waiter, by the way."

The waiter said no problem. He left us alone for another half hour while Daisy ate a bite of ice cream, followed by a spoonful of fudge sauce, followed by one nut, et cetera. Her spoon moved methodically back and forth among the two plates and the cup of fudge sauce until only the cherry was left.

"It all gets mixed together again in your stomach, you know," I reminded her.

Daisy sliced the cherry in half.

"Take your time," I said. "I happen to have had a particularly stinky day, but don't let that bother you. It happens to have been because of your silly secret, which I have a right to know, but don't let that bother you either. Who am I to complain?"

"You're the world's champion complainer — that's who you are," said Gratkins. "But don't let that bother you."

She began bringing Daisy up to date on that morning's episode of "One Life to Live," but for once Daisy wasn't interested. "I'd like to know yours, too," she said.

"Know my what?" I asked.

"Your secret." Daisy poked her fork into half of the cherry. "Like who you are and why you're in my house."

Who *I* am? Why I'm in *her* house? She had some nerve! "You show me your birth certificate, and I'll show you mine," I suggested angrily.

Daisy confessed that she'd made up the story about the birth certificate to get us out of trouble. "You've been nice to me," she told Gratkins. "Now tell me who you are."

Gratkins didn't answer. She just sat there looking worried while Daisy cut that half cherry into seven tiny pieces. And ate one. And chewed it for an eon.

"I think we should go," I said.

Daisy said, "I haven't finished eating."

She ate two more bites of cherry before putting down her fork. "Who are you?" she demanded. "I want to know."

Gratkins started to fuss with the check, figuring out the tip and counting coins. Then she looked around the room as if she were in a hurry to get that waiter back again.

"I want to know," Daisy repeated in a voice so soft that I could barely hear.

It struck me that the conversation was getting heavy. Scary, even. I looked at Gratkins, wondering if she had heard Daisy's question. When I saw her face, I knew she had.

"Well?" said Daisy.

Gratkins sighed. Then she looked Daisy straight in the eye and said, "I'm you."

It was like one of those saloon scenes in Westerns where the good guy and the bad guy have it out while everyone else freezes. What did Gratkins mean? What was going on?

"Give me a break!" I said.

They both ignored me. "I was afraid to let you know," Gratkins told Daisy. "I was afraid you wouldn't like me. Like yourself, that is. The self that lives in the future you slid into, down that laundry chute in 1943."

I stood up so fast that my chair fell over backward. "Can we go home now?" I asked. "I don't feel well, so can we please go home?"

I was desperate, but did anybody listen? Dream

on! The waiter reappeared to take the check. Daisy took a brush out of her book bag and brushed her hair, which is a disgusting thing to do in an ice cream parlor. Gratkins blotted her lipstick with a napkin.

"First we have to stop by Computer Shack," she said. "They called this morning to say that Daisy's laptop was ready."

There's a moral to this chapter. Here it is: What happens when your whole world falls apart? Life goes on!

Chapter 7

When I walked into English class the next morning, I had the surprise of my life. Mrs. Magorian took me aside and actually smiled. Or at least she clenched her teeth and pushed her mouth out toward her ears.

I felt like saying "That's better, Mrs. Magorian! See what you can do when you make an effort?"

I didn't, though. I kept my own mouth shut and listened while she told me how pleased she was about our little conference yesterday because it gave her some insight on my family situation.

"I want you to know that from now on, I'm giving you a free hand with your autobiography," she went on.

I said, "Thanks, Mrs. Magorian."

"And whenever you feel the need to verbalize your antagonisms, you're welcome to go into the computer room and use one of the machines."

"Verbalize my antagonisms?" I echoed.

"Yes, dear. It's natural to resent the arrival of a new sibling. Especially when that sibling is a twin."

I hate it when a grown-up starts talking like a book. I told her I didn't have any antagonisms — I just had a sister who acted like a jerk. If I could trade Daisy for a brother, life would be a bowl of roses. But Mrs. Magorian practiced her smile some more and said she understood and please not to bring food or drink into the computer room.

"And I promise not to peek until the end of the month when it's time for you girls to share your SWAP projects," she added.

I thanked her again. Not that I have the slightest intention of letting her read it even then. At least not all of it. Because what I've found out since that conference would put my family in headlines the world over if Mrs. Magorian found out about it, too.

I took her up on her offer to spend extra time in the computer room, though. That's why I'm here during recess. It's Monday the twenty-second, a warm day for November, and everyone else is outside. I'd like to be outside myself, but I have too much to tell.

For instance, the salesman didn't charge us for fixing Daisy's laptop. In the first place, it was under warranty. In the second place, it was in perfect shape except for a pierced-earring stud that he fished out from under the keyboard. He shamed Gratkins into buying a plastic dust cover that Daisy won't use because it's tacky, but he didn't shame her into signing a contract for the service plan. Daisy drifted off toward the rack with the adventure games and didn't hear a word the man was saying. But I was right there listening, and I didn't like what I heard.

What mainly annoyed me was his attitude. He was

a real geek. The kind who turns himself off with the rest of the computers at closing time. Or, as Daisy's laptop manual would put it, spends the night in standby mode to avoid superfluous consumption of battery power. The whole time he was talking to Gratkins, he had this condescending smile on his face, as if he were dealing with a total moron.

"Tell your daughter to read the manual," he said.

"My *granddaughter* is right here," Gratkins told him. "Both my granddaughters are here. They're Academy students, and they know their way around a computer. Yours was malfunctioning."

The salesman's smile became even more condescending. "Really? It was working smoothly again by the time it arrived in the shop."

"You mean you didn't fix it?" I asked.

"There was nothing to fix," he said. "Would you be interested in our *Beginner's Quick Reference Guide*, designed to help you familiarize yourself with your new computer?"

I said, "No, thanks."

It was Daisy's computer, not mine, but I didn't tell him that. I didn't want him anywhere near Daisy after what I had heard at the restaurant. If she was really from 1943, she didn't want the laptop giving her secret away. Leaving the salesman with Gratkins, I slipped off to tell her so.

"Keep your distance," I warned her. "You don't want that man to know what's going on."

"What *is* going on?" asked Daisy. She had loaded a trial game on *This Week's Hardware Special* and was having a fine old time. "I haven't lost yet!" she said happily. "Only I can't understand why I'm not winning either."

"It's because you haven't started the game yet," I told her. "That's the options screen you're playing around with. You have to select the right one in order to default to keyboard, and then you can begin. Like this. See?"

"No," said Daisy, and she gave me a blank, hazeleyed stare.

"Forget it," I said. "Let's go home. There are some questions I need to ask."

And boy, did I ever ask questions! Like what did Gratkins mean when she said she was Daisy? One and the same person? That was impossible! I could believe that Daisy had arrived out of the past; it explained her weird behavior. But if Gratkins was Daisy grown up, how could they both be here at once?

Daisy just shook her head when I asked. She seemed totally stunned. But Gratkins made an effort to explain.

"That laundry chute claims to take you fifty years ahead of your time, remember? It gives you a new lease on life."

"Okay," I conceded. "So it's a time warp. But that doesn't account for *you*. If Daisy slid into a new life, how come you stayed behind and grew up the normal way?"

Gratkins said she didn't know. "My guess is that it's not a time warp, though. I think it's more like a time *stutter*. I didn't get moved, I just got duplicated."

All I can say is, Daisy sure doesn't look like a duplicated Gratkins. She's smart and pretty, and she's young. She has half a century before she reaches sixty-three. When she finally does, will she look the way Gratkins looks today?

I could tell that Daisy was wondering the same thing. I didn't envy her. "How did you happen to slide down the chute in the first place?" I asked, to get her mind off the dilemma.

Gratkins said, "You tell, Daisy. For you it's not so long ago."

Daisy thought for a moment. "I was born here in this house," she began. "That was back in 1930. And the party when we were playing Sardines was in 1943."

I've often played Sardines myself. In fact, Gratkins taught me. It's like a backward hide-and-seek: the person who's "it" is the one to hide, and all the others try to find him. When they do, they crawl in and hide with him. Pretty soon you're packed together like a can of sardines, and the last one in is the next to be "it."

"You mean you hid in the laundry chute?" I asked.

Daisy shook her head. "I hid in the linen closet. I was 'it,' and Edwin was the first to find me."

"Who was Edwin?"

"Edwin's my older brother," Daisy and Gratkins answered in unison. They looked at each other and laughed, only Daisy's laugh was a little woebegone.

"Edwin was a bully," Gratkins explained. "He grew nicer as he grew older, but for a while, he was a real terror. That party must have been at the end of July because it was for his fifteenth birthday. Old enough to know better, you might say!"

71

"It was the twenty-fourth of July," I reminded her. "The day Daisy came out of the chute was, anyway."

"Fifty years to the day," Gratkins said with a pensive look on her face. She seemed to be doing mental arithmetic while Daisy went on talking.

"He pinched me!" said Daisy. "He had this way of pinching the skin inside my arm, just above the elbow. The soft part, where it hurts, and —"

Gratkins picked up her story. "— and I tried to escape down the laundry chute, but Edwin caught me by my sash. Later he boasted that he'd saved my life. He ruined the dress, though. My mother had to cut it up for rags."

Daisy was surprised. "What do you mean? He didn't catch *me*. *My* dress wasn't ruined."

"That's when you and I parted ways," said Gratkins. "The dress must have been duplicated, too."

A shiver ran through me. "No wonder your parents nailed up the laundry chute!"

"They should have, then and there," Gratkins agreed. "But they didn't actually get around to it until a few months later."

"You're kidding! Why did they wait?"

"Because the chute was so convenient. They thought it would be enough to make the linen closet out of bounds, as I recall. But they caught Edwin on the point of sliding down that chute himself, the following December. There was a terrible fuss, and they finally boarded it up."

"About time!" I said, but Gratkins ignored me.

"So you escaped," she murmured, peering into Daisy's face as if it held the story of her own past. "When Edwin saved my life, you were taken fifty years ahead of your time."

Daisy frowned. "It's funny you think Edwin saved your life, because personally, I think he pushed me in. It wouldn't have been the first time, after all."

"He tried it before, did he? I don't remember that."

"I don't remember it either," said Daisy. "It happened long ago, one spring when I was two years old. But Mama says she caught Edwin just in time. She says he was holding the flap open and about to drop me in."

"So that's what happened," Gratkins said thoughtfully. "What a little horror Edwin was!"

They both got a laugh out of this, but there were tears in Daisy's eyes as she asked, "Where's Mama?"

"She had a long, happy life," Gratkins reassured her. "She was eighty-seven when she died."

Was this my great-grandmother they were talking about? Then my so-called twin sister was really my grandmother, and Gratkins was, too.

"I don't know if I can handle this," I said. "I'm tired. Maybe I'll skip supper tonight and just have a sandwich in bed."

Daisy said she was tired, too, and she'd have hers in front of the TV. Then at least other people would be talking instead of us. But Gratkins said no, we needed each other more than ever, and we should have a formal, family dinner.

Formal dinner was a new one for me. I reminded

her that there's no table in our dining room. In fact, there's no furniture at all. But she said to clear off a table in the living room and set out the last of the silver knives and forks. We ate off Wedgwood plates: the chipped ones that Gratkins hadn't sold. Want to know what we ate? Hamburgers and baked potatoes — that's what. One result of that nightmare conference was no more shepherd's pie. When Mrs. Magorian told her what I wrote about it, Gratkins gave up. Not that it really matters, now that I have a dog to eat the meat. But it proves that when all else fails, writing is a means of communication.

The whole time we were eating, I stared at Daisy and Gratkins, trying to find a resemblance in their faces. All I could see was the hazel eyes and the shadow of a dimple in their chins. But those things must run in the family, because I have them, too. I was sorry for Daisy. In her place, I'd feel as if I didn't belong to myself anymore. So I helped with the dishes even though it was her night to do them, and helped again later with her math. Daisy may be good in English, but she's a klutz at math.

Gratkins always reads the paper while Daisy and I do our homework. That evening, she kept interrupting with our horoscope.

"The planets are lined up for a hot romance this week," she informed us. "Business ventures are a bummer for Scorpios until the twenty-ninth. We should resist the temptation to spread ourselves too thin. How about if we spread ourselves into bed and make it an early night?"

"Could I spread myself into Daisy's room?" I asked.

I counted on Daisy to back me up since I'd been so nice to her. But all she said was, "Tonight's show has been canceled due to popular demand."

"Which means what?" I asked.

"Which means no way. You snore."

This is untrue, and Daisy knows it. She wasn't worried about snoring when she came creeping into my room later, carrying her pillow and the flouncy quilt. I sleep so soundly that practically nothing wakes me up, so I didn't notice until she tried to get into my bed. I might not have noticed even then if Laptop hadn't started growling. He was under the covers and didn't want company.

"What do you think you're doing?" I asked. "What time is it, anyway?"

"Two o'clock," Daisy said. "I couldn't sleep."

"Is that any reason to wake *me* up?" I demanded. "Neither of us will sleep if we share this bed. It isn't wide enough."

We shared it, though. After I kicked Laptop out, Daisy and I slept like two logs until my alarm went off. But first she told me what was bothering her.

"I keep getting myself mixed up with the Daisy back in 1943," she explained. "Then I start thinking that no matter what she does, she'll grow up to be Gratkins."

"What's wrong with that?" I asked defensively. "Gratkins is nice."

Daisy agreed. "Still, if the 1943 Daisy and I are

the same person — and I know we are — then it doesn't matter what I do from now on, because I'll grow up to be Gratkins anyway. See what I mean?"

"Gratkins is already grown up," I reminded her. "This is 1993. That party, with the game of Sardines and everything, is way back in the past."

Daisy gave a little shiver and wiggled so close that she almost shoved me out of bed. "We were born in 1930. Gratkins is sixty-three now. Am I sixty-three or thirteen?"

"Thirteen," I said. "Don't let your imagination run away with you. Just shut up and go to sleep."

Daisy yawned. "Yes, but Garet — say Gratkins dies when she's a hundred."

"Go to sleep, Daisy," I repeated.

"That'll be in the year 2030," Daisy went on, ignoring me. "If I'm only thirteen, I'll be fifty then. But if I'm really Gratkins, maybe I'll be a hundred, too. Except if I only look fifty, maybe I'll live on until I look a hundred, which would be in 2080. When of course I'd really be a hundred and fifty."

I groaned. "If you don't go to sleep, you'll look a hundred and fifty tomorrow morning."

"Yes, but Garet — what if I die when Gratkins dies?"

"She's not going to die," I told her. "She's going to live to be a hundred, remember?"

"I just said that to make the arithmetic easier," said Daisy. "She's already sixty-three. She might die tomorrow."

"She won't," I promised. "Daisy, would you please shut up?"

"Okay," said Daisy, but she didn't. Instead she sat up and whimpered, "I don't want to be Gratkins. If she dies tomorrow, I might die, too."

"If she dies tomorrow, I wouldn't want to be Gratkins either," I said, and I rolled over and went to sleep.

Daisy says she went right to sleep then, too, so maybe I just dreamed that she was crying.

Chapter 8

Mrs. Magorian has just made it perfectly clear that she doesn't believe this is the true story of my life. She doesn't even believe it's the true Daisy Atkins Story. Except for the part about Daisy's embarrassing birth certificate, which happens to be the least true thing about it.

"We'll just call it fictionalized autobiography," she said kindly.

That kind of kindness I don't need. "Fictionalized autobiography" was just a polite way of calling me a liar, which is more than a self-respecting person can stand. But if I want to protect my family, I can't offer to prove that any of this is true. Any of what she read up until the conference, that is. She's only guessing what I've written since the end of chapter five.

I sat at my computer for a while, brooding over the fix I was in. Meanwhile, Mrs. Magorian hovered over me with her new mouth-stretching smile. She got on my nerves. I switched to brooding over how to make her go away.

"Okay," I conceded. "Maybe some of what people say isn't in the exact same words. But the *things* they say are true."

Mrs. Magorian bobbed her head eagerly as if a slow student had finally made a quarter inch of progress. "That's an interesting observation, Garet. To what extent is the chronicler of actual events permitted to interpret or improvise?"

Sometimes I wonder if Mrs. Magorian's mind works like a sieve and lets simple words through while it keeps back the ones with lots of syllables. "What does that mean?" I asked.

"The Professional Author knows how to edit a conversation while still retaining the essence of it," she went on. "To include every little 'well' or 'uh' would make dialogue unbearably tedious. I'm glad to see you are aware of the problem. But editing is one thing and embellishment is another. You mustn't let your imagination run away with you."

She's wrong about imagination. A runaway imagination is often the only thing that can save you. In our family, thank goodness, imaginations don't just run. They gallop! I say "thank goodness" because otherwise, I don't know what we would have done about Daisy's birth certificate.

It was Daisy herself who brought the subject up last night at supper. "We were supposed to give it to Mrs. Magorian today," she reminded Gratkins.

Gratkins got that worried look on her face again. "Oh, dear! Couldn't we just let it slide?"

"We could," Daisy agreed. "But if she remembers, it would draw even more attention to us than before."

I told them they were a couple of dreamers. "If Mrs. Magorian remembers? Of course she'll remember! She's *drooling* to find out what's so embarrassing about Daisy's birth certificate."

Gratkins shuddered. "Who knows what sordid thoughts that woman has in her head?"

"I do," Daisy said, blushing. "She thinks I'm illegitimate — that's what. She thinks my parents were never married."

"That's nonsense!" I told her. "You're behind the times. Fifty years behind the times, to be exact. I could name you half a dozen kids at Whetstone whose parents never got married. It's not embarrassing — it's classy."

Daisy looked interested. "Classy like anchorwomen?"

"Not quite," I said. "Anyway, don't get your hopes up. If you're illegitimate, then I am, too, and my birth certificate is already on file, right?"

Gratkins curled her mouth into a sly smile. "Wrong. Run and get my handbag, Garet."

I got her the bag, and wouldn't you know it — there was a copy of my birth certificate inside.

"Gratkins!" I wailed. "Did you snitch this out of my file? Now we're really in trouble!"

"No such thing," she said. "On the contrary, it was smart thinking on my part. There's a place to check off if there's more than one child born. Good your teacher didn't notice! We'll check it now, and all our troubles will be over."

"What do you mean?" I asked, watching her make

a careful mark in the right box. "We still have to send in a copy of Daisy's certificate, don't we? And we have to think of something embarrassing that could happen to just one twin. Like maybe she was born without a mind."

Instead of laughing, Gratkins sighed and said that the Academy wouldn't go for a mindless Daisy, but perhaps we'd come up with an idea by the time we got to the drugstore.

"Why the drugstore?"

"To copy your birth certificate, of course," Gratkins explained. "You're twins, so the two documents would be similar. Besides, any little adjustments I may have made will be less noticeable in a copy."

It occurred to me that my grandmother was slightly off her rocker. Sure, the documents would be similar. But not identical.

"Wait just a minute!" I said. "We can't copy my birth certificate. It's got *my name* on it."

Daisy and Gratkins stared innocently at me. Were they just pretending to be stupid?

"We're getting into major forgery here," I told them impatiently. "How are you going to change Garet into Daisy?"

"Margaret," Gratkins corrected me gently.

"What do you mean, Margaret?"

"The name on your certificate is Margaret, honey. You were named for me, remember?"

She was right. It's something I haven't mentioned before because Margaret is not a name I'm fond of. Gratkins says she always liked it, but that's because

81

no one ever called her Margarine, like some kids at Whetstone used to call me. That's why I began to use Garet for short.

"Okay, so how are you going to change Margaret into Daisy?" I demanded.

"I don't have to," said Gratkins. "Daisy is a nick-name for Margaret — didn't you know? It's because of *marguerite*, which means daisy in French."

It sounded kind of farfetched to me, but she argued that Daisy had been her own nickname when she was a teenager, so she should know.

"Don't worry, Mrs. Magorian will understand," she said decisively.

"Maybe," I said, "but we can't both be named for you. People at the Academy think it's strange already, that this so-called twin turns up out of nowhere. What are they going to think when they find out we're both named Margaret? You can't do this to me. I mean, it'll be really embarrassing!"

"Embarrassing," Gratkins echoed. "That solves our problem."

In other words, I had found the embarrassing thing about Daisy's birth certificate. It was *me*. But I shouldn't complain, because Mrs. Magorian swallowed the story hook, line, and sinker. I returned from slipping my own birth certificate back into the office file just in time to hear her say, "Twin sisters with the same name? How quaint! I've never heard of parents doing that before. Of course, it would have to be a name like Margaret with its multiple nick-names."

"That's right," Daisy agreed, with a mischievous

82

glance at me. "Before our parents decided on Garet, they nearly called her Margarine."

Thank goodness that passed right over Mrs. Magorian's head. "You don't say!" she murmured. "Well, let's be thankful that you girls are together at last with a loving, caring grandmother to make a home for you. And someday when we have time, I want you to sit down and tell me the story of how you came to be separated in the first place."

Mrs. Magorian is unpredictable. Next thing you know, she'll be *begging* me for fictionalized autobiography. Fortunately she has her hands full with the other students in 7-B. Ever since she asked for mood, they've been cramming their autobiographies so full of it that there's no room left for the story of their lives. The one whose mood is passionate has been using language that's not allowed at Whetstone Academy. Mrs. Magorian has to censor it, so she spends a lot of time standing behind that girl's back with *Roget's Thesaurus*.

I know who it is now. I've even read some of it. And I don't believe for a minute that a love-crazed duke ripped Staci Farnham's bodice off. Staci doesn't know any love-crazed dukes, and she has never worn a bodice. In my opinion, she doesn't even know what a bodice is. I'm not sure myself, but I plan to find out from Gratkins tonight at supper.

Chapter 9

Something totally mind-blowing happened in the attic last night while Gratkins was out playing bridge. You won't get it in this chapter, though. I'm saving it for chapter ten. Wouldn't The Professional Author be proud of me? I'll lead up to it slowly, starting with a conversation in the car.

Gratkins was driving us home from school yesterday, as usual. And as usual, she was bringing Daisy up to date on the soaps. She had finished "The Young and the Restless" and was just starting on "As the World Turns" when Daisy interrupted her.

"What's corroboration?" she asked, right out of the blue.

Her question reminded me of Staci Farnham's autobiography. So before Gratkins had time to open her mouth, I brought up the other problem word. "While you're at it, what's a bodice?"

"One you wear and one you don't," Gratkins answered without even stopping to think.

"Come on, be serious!" I said.

Gratkins explained that a bodice is a sort of corset, and corroboration is support.

"Like an underwire bra?" Daisy asked.

Gratkins thought this was pretty funny. In fact, she laughed so hard that she had to pull over to the side of the road and calm down before she could go on driving. But after she left for her bridge party, Daisy and I checked both words in the dictionary.

" 'Bodice: a piece of clothing that a woman wears above the waist,' " I read. "Staci Farnham has a dirty mind!"

Daisy said it was probably one of those tight vest things with laces like what Snow White wears. "You couldn't expect a love-crazed duke to untie laces," she reasoned. "Now look up *corroboration*. A bra doesn't make sense — I think it's something to do with photographs."

I asked why she wanted to know, and she explained that it was for SWAP. The girls in 7-A have been interviewing each other like newspaper reporters. Now they have to turn the interviews into articles. Today Mrs. Magorian told them to bring in snapshots of themselves as kids, to use as corroboration.

"Then for sure she doesn't mean a bra," I said, flipping ahead to *C* in the dictionary. "It says here that to corroborate is to confirm something, or make it valid."

Daisy looked worried. "I can't do that! The pictures of me are too old-fashioned. And it's too late to change all the stuff I told my interviewer."

When I heard what she told her interviewer, I was

scandalized. I mean, it's one thing to hide the truth out of self-protection and another to invent a pack of lies. Daisy told this girl that she had been stolen from her cradle by a demented hospital nurse who locked her up in a closet where Daisy was forced to work like a slave. According to her story, it had taken the combined efforts of Gratkins and the FBI twelve years to track her down.

"What a heartwarming story!" I said. "What kind of work did you do, locked up in that closet?"

Before Daisy could answer, I lost my temper. "Of all the idiotic, feeble-minded jerks, you take the prize! Didn't it occur to you that we were in trouble enough after Mrs. Magorian read my autobiography? You had to go and make it worse?"

Daisy said it was too late to change her story now, so would I please stop trying to make her feel guilty and think up a way to help instead. "I need some photographs," she said. "What am I going to do?"

I pretended to think hard. "How about if we just cut out a few scenes from a horror comic?"

"Photographs," Daisy repeated humorlessly. "There's a whole bunch up in the attic, but they won't do."

"Use some of mine," I said. "There aren't any from before I came to live here, but there's a cute one of me the day I moved in, when I was two. I'm wearing an old-fashioned lace dress with puffed sleeves. It's on Gratkins's bedside table."

Daisy shook her head. "I told you, old-fashioned won't do."

"Well, how about something really modern,

then?" I suggested. "Like you at the age of sixty-three, for instance. We could ask Gratkins for the one off her driver's license."

Daisy was on the edge of tears, so I stopped teasing and said we should go up to the attic and look for photos after supper.

The reason I said *after* supper is that supper last night was pizza, which I happen to adore. When Gratkins goes out to a bridge party, she always orders pizza and rents a video for me and Daisy. She says it's so we can have a good time, too. We never watched the video last night, though. Instead we took the pizza into my room so we could get our homework out of the way and leave the rest of the evening free for exploring the attic.

"I'll do your English if you'll do my math," Daisy offered, dropping her book bag on my floor.

"No, thanks," I said.

"Could you at least help me with it?" she asked. "I hate math! Why on earth would anyone want to know that '*v* equals *pi-r*-squared-*h* over three,' for instance?"

"It's for if they want to know the volume of a cone," I told her. "I'll eat your mushrooms if you'll eat my sausage."

"No, thanks," she said. "If you need to know the volume of a cone, watch the man at Baskin Robbins. It looks like a lot on top, but inside the cone is empty because he's too stingy to pack the ice cream down."

"Very funny," I said. "It's too bad you hate math. Gratkins and I both like it."

Daisy looked surprised. "Gratkins likes math? No

kidding! I wonder what's going to happen to make me change my mind?"

Her question made me feel really uncomfortable. How could she stand knowing what she'd be like when she grew up? It must take all the surprise out of life! Maybe that's what Gratkins meant when we were in the hospital, waiting for Daisy to be stitched up last August. Not many people would want to be Daisy and share a house with their own future.

I glanced at Daisy's face to see if she was having the same disturbing thought, but Daisy was performing open-heart surgery on her pizza. "Gratkins knows I don't like onions," she grumbled. "Why do you suppose she ordered them?"

"Because *I* like them. Just scrape them off."

They were already off, of course. When Daisy eats pizza, she has to put her slice on a tray so there's room for all the little heaps of toppings. She even separates the cheese from the tomato sauce. After each bite of the basic pizza, she picks up a topping between her pinky and her thumb and delicately pops it in her mouth. This amuses the other customers when we're in a restaurant, but it drives me crazy.

"I should write a description of the way you eat," I said. "The American Medical Association might pay good money for it."

You'd think Daisy would be embarrassed, but she's totally insensitive to this kind of comment. "Couldn't you please, please do my math for me?" she begged. "I just remembered I still have to do my English."

I told her I thought her English homework was finding corroboration in the attic, but she said no, that didn't count. "We have to write a letter to an author. I'm writing mine to Ernest Hemingway."

"What on earth for?" I asked.

Daisy explained how the girls in 7-A are reading *The Old Man and the Sea* and how it's beginning to drag on a bit. "I'm going to ask him to set his next story on dry land," she said. "Should I send it care of his publisher?"

"Send it care of God," I suggested.

Daisy couldn't believe that Hemingway was dead. "He's such a promising young writer!" she wailed. "What happened?"

"I guess he grew into a promising *old* writer," I said. "This is 1993, remember?"

I'll never figure out which things bother Daisy, and which ones don't. Why should the mention of some dead author make her look so mournful? "Cheer up," I said. "He wrote a lot of good books during that time. He was famous."

Daisy shook her head. "Who cares about Hemingway? It's Gratkins that I mind about. It's not fair that she got to live through all those years, and I had to skip over them."

So she was jealous, not mournful. What could I say? Daisy got a rotten deal in my opinion, and there was nothing either one of us could do about it.

Daisy scooped up her onions and fed them to Laptop, who was polite but not what you'd call grateful. "It's having no choice that I mind," she told me.

"What if I want to go on hating math? When I grow up, do I have to like it just because something made Gratkins start liking it?"

I gave her question real thought. "I don't know," I said finally. "If you like it, you'll like liking it, though."

"Gratkins probably ate the way I do when she was thirteen," Daisy continued in a gloomy voice. "That means something will happen to make me like food when it's mixed together. Yuck! I hope it doesn't happen soon."

"If you like it, you won't think 'yuck,' " I reasoned. "That's the whole point. Shut up and finish your math homework."

Daisy was too upset to concentrate on math, so I gave in and helped after all. It's good I did; she was making a real mess of it. "You'll have to do a heap of changing before you get good at math," I told her. "Squared doesn't mean times two, dummy! It means you multiply something by itself."

Instead of learning from me, Daisy wandered over to the shelf where I keep my pig collection. I have over fifty pigs, ranging from a big pink plush one to a tiny silver one the size of my thumbnail. My favorite is a china piglet with rosebuds all over it.

"Watch out!" I said when Daisy picked one up. "Some of those are fragile."

"I'm just putting them in order," Daisy said, and she started to line them up like soldiers.

Of course it wouldn't occur to Daisy that not everyone wants her pig collection to look like a military parade. Not everyone wants every single pig facing the same direction. Not everyone is neat to the point of lunacy. I heaved a meaningful sigh, but Daisy kept right at it.

She was getting on my nerves. "Write your letter to Hemingway if you're bored," I advised her. "Why should I do your math while you're messing up my pigs?"

"They were already a mess," she said, reaching for my china piglet.

"So leave them that way!" I snapped—and she dropped it.

I told earlier how Daisy's room is full of things: old clothes and books and toys that she brought down from the attic. I may be messy, but I don't happen to collect things the way she does. Only pigs. And I do happen to love my pigs. Each one has a story behind it. I could tell you where it came from, how old it is, and how it's made. Each one also has a private name, although I'm getting a little old for that. So when the tail broke off the china piglet, I got mad.

"Dumb klutz!" I shouted.

Daisy said she was sorry, but I could tell she didn't really care.

"That was my favorite, and you ruined it," I moaned. "I bet you did it on purpose!"

That's when Daisy got mad. She said she hadn't done it on purpose, but she wished she had. "It's not yours, anyway," she added. "Gratkins had no right to give it to you, because it belongs to me."

It's true that some of my things belonged to Gratkins long ago. That means they used to belong to Daisy, and I can see how she might want them back. Not the piglet, though. If there's one thing in the house that's really mine, it's the piglet. It happens to have been in the pocket of that old-fashioned lace dress with puffed sleeves that I wore the day I moved in, when I was two. But when I told Daisy this, she said I was lying.

"*Me* lying?" I said. "*You're* the liar!"

"It belongs to me," she repeated angrily. "You're not just a liar, you're a thief!"

She grabbed the piglet and threw it against the wall where it smashed to smithereens. So what did I do? I'm not ashamed to admit it. I slapped Daisy.

It's a funny thing about fights. While they're going on, all you want is to make the other person admit they're wrong. Say they're really sorry. Cry. But if they do, you feel terrible. And Daisy did.

"I'm sorry, Daisy!" I said. "God, I'm really sorry — I don't know what made me do that."

So even though she was wrong, I'm the one who apologized. You figure it! In any case, I spent the next hour trying to get her to stop crying. I finished her math. I wrote her letter to Ernest Hemingway. Then I began thinking that an hour is an awfully long time to cry over one measly slap, so I asked her what was really wrong. Get this: she was homesick!

"We've been through this before," I reminded her. "Two weeks ago it made sense, but not now. This *is* your home."

Daisy had a hard time talking through her sobs. I had to make her repeat herself once or twice before I understood that she missed her brothers and sisters.

"Even Edwin?" I asked.

"Even Edwin." Daisy got down on her hands and knees and started picking up bits of piglet. She wasn't crying anymore, but from time to time she sniffed and wiped her nose with the back of her hand. In my opinion, there aren't many things Daisy and I have in common, but looking awful when we cry is one of them.

Suddenly she jumped up again. "Where are the boar and the sow?"

"Where are who?" I began to wonder if I should call up Gratkins at her bridge party. Daisy was acting really weird. She made less and less sense, each new thing she said.

"The other china pigs," said Daisy. "There used to be three of them."

I told her I didn't know what she was talking about. According to Gratkins, I arrived in her house with just the piglet in my pocket. "It was an orphan piglet," I said. "It never had any parents."

"It did so!" said Daisy. "There was a mother and a father, and I want to know what happened to them."

"Somebody turned them into bacon, maybe," I said. "Who cares?"

Daisy started crying again. "I care, that's who. It's fine for you. You don't remember your parents, so you don't miss them. I lived with mine until July, and now Gratkins tells me they've been dead for thirty years."

"So how does that make it worse for you?" I demanded. "Yours have been dead for thirty years and mine for just eleven. I should mind more than you, because it happened more recently."

It struck me that for once, we were arguing about something worthwhile. Which is worse: to love people and have them die or to not remember whether you loved them in the first place? I assumed Daisy was asking herself the same question, because she stopped crying and got this speculative look on her face.

"Are you thinking the same thing I'm thinking?" I asked.

"Yes," said Daisy.

But it turned out she wasn't. Wiping her nose on her hand one final time, she grinned and said, "I wonder who I married."

Chapter 10

I'm ready to tell you what happened in the attic now, but guess what? There isn't time.

Mrs. Magorian just came into the computer room and said I have exactly five minutes to shut off the computer. What's more, I won't get to use it again until next Monday. Four whole days — what a bummer! Why? Thanksgiving. What with all the excitement about Daisy being Gratkins, I forgot something I've never forgotten before in my whole entire life: a school vacation. It starts today at noon, but if you think I'm grateful, think again.

"I wouldn't have known you were still in here if Daisy hadn't told me," Mrs. Magorian said. Then she added, "It's lovely to see how you're finally getting to know your sister."

"Getting to know Daisy?" I said. "I know all I want to know about her."

Mrs. Magorian said there were different ways of knowing people. "Take you, for instance, Garet. I've known you to say hello to since your first year at

Whetstone. I've known you as my English student since September. But I know you in a new and better way through your autobiography."

Which she had promised not to read until it was finished, right? I glanced up at her face to see if she was cheating and reading over my shoulder. From where I sat, her new smile looked faker than ever. It made me mad. Who does she think she is, saying she knows me?

"Knock, knock!" I said.

"Who's there?" asked Mrs. Magorian, adding a touch of cute to her new smile.

"See what I mean?" I said.

She looked totally baffled.

"Whoops!" I said. "I forgot the first part of the joke."

Believe me, though, it's no joke. Mrs. Magorian doesn't know me. I don't know Daisy. And sometimes I wonder if Gratkins knows either of her so-called granddaughters.

Why *so-called?*

(To be continued.)

Chapter 11

I know I promised to write what happened in the attic, but first I want it on record that I'm worried about Daisy. She's not acting like herself, whoever that is.

Here's where The Intelligent Reader says, "Hold it! Daisy is Gratkins, right?"

Wrong! At least, wrong according to Daisy. Ever since the night last week when we went through the photos in the attic, she's been dead certain she isn't Gratkins after all. What's more, she's out to prove it. How? By comparing their fingerprints, of all things!

"Won't that hurt Gratkins's feelings?" I asked.

"Not if I play my cards right," said Daisy.

Today is Monday, our first day back after vacation. By some miracle, Daisy was ready for school ahead of schedule. I was a little startled to see her wearing the peach-colored party dress that she came down the laundry chute in. It's not your typical anchorwoman outfit, and she knew as well as I did that it wouldn't go over big at Whetstone. Why was she wearing it, then? I soon found out.

"You're wearing *our dress!*" Gratkins said, blushing with pleasure when Daisy appeared in the kitchen.

Daisy was so early that she actually sat down to eat something. Namely cornflakes with milk. And you guessed it, she ate each spoonful of cornflakes dry, followed by a sip of milk. You'll never catch Daisy pouring one on top of the other. That's why she doesn't usually have time for breakfast. But this morning she even had time left over to play her cards right. The conversation went like this:

Gratkins:	"Daisy, you look positively scrumptious this morning!"
Daisy:	"Thanks! I'm counting on *our dress* to bring me luck."
Gratkins:	"Why do you need luck? Do you have a test today?"
Daisy:	"No. It's just I'm hoping not to get detention during sports again, like last Wednesday."
Gratkins:	"Heavens! I didn't know you got detention Wednesday. What happened, wasn't your homework done on time?"
Daisy:	"Oh, no! It's just I forgot to bring something to school. Well [here she bats her eyelashes, believe it or not] I didn't actually forget. It's more like I didn't dare ask you for it."

Gratkins:	"Maybe you better tell me what that thing is."
Daisy:	"First of all I need five dollars."
Gratkins:	"But sweetheart, you know I give you school money whenever you need it!"
Daisy:	"Yes, but you pay for so much already, and it's not like you really wanted me in your life or anything."
Garet:	[Awed silence. When Daisy plays her cards right, I tend to get choked up with a mixture of envy and disgust. She has managed to set things up so that now Gratkins will agree to anything. Anything!]
Gratkins:	"How can you say such a thing? The day you came here was one of the happiest days of my life. Why, I'd do anything for you, Daisy — anything!"
Garet:	[Nauseated silence. Can you believe this? And I swear it's word for word!]
Gratkins:	"You said 'first of all.' What else were you embarrassed to ask me for?"
Daisy:	"Your fingerprints. Garet won't let me do hers. She says it's messy."
Garet:	[Angry silence. She never asked me, to begin with. But what I really mind is that she's using

me. I don't happen to like being used.]

Gratkins: "Why would you want to take Garet's fingerprints?"

Daisy: "The science teacher wants them for a study on twins. Could I use yours instead? They'd be better than Garet's anyway because she and I aren't really twins. But you and I are the same person, *right?*"

I've been wondering about something for quite some time now. How come Daisy is such a manipulator when Gratkins is the soul of honor? If you ask me, that's a much bigger change than from hating math to liking math. In fact, I'm tempted to ask Gratkins about it. I'll say, "When did you quit being such a scummy little liar?"

Gratkins is not stupid. She can always tell when *I'm* trying to put something over on her. So I expected her to laugh in Daisy's face. Instead she turned kind of pale and said, "Oh, dear! I should have thought of that."

Daisy looked triumphant. She obviously felt this proved that she and Gratkins weren't the same person. She said in a whiny voice that no one could force Gratkins to have her fingerprints taken if she had some private reason not to. She added that it wasn't so bad being on detention because that way she could get her homework done and didn't have to wear her barf-green gym suit.

"So forget it," she finished.

Gratkins said by no means would she forget it. She hadn't the least objection to having her fingerprints taken. In fact, she'd enjoy it. "Don't let your teacher get hold of Garet's real prints though," she said. "It would just make trouble."

Are twins supposed to have identical fingerprints or something? I'll have to ask the science teacher. I'll save it for a time when I want to give Daisy a good scare. Which may be soon, because I don't like the way she plays around with Gratkins's feelings.

"That fingerprint business was a dirty trick," I told her after we had been dropped off at school. "Gratkins really loves you. You know how mushy she got when she saw you in that dress this morning. What are you going to do — run in and say, 'Hey, wow! Guess what? We're not even related!' Don't you care how she feels?"

"If Gratkins and I are the same person, she feels the same way I do, doesn't she?" Daisy reasoned slyly.

I didn't quite agree with this. It was time for morning assembly, however, so I dropped the subject. Instead I asked Daisy what the five dollars were for.

"Staci Farnham's little brother has a detective kit," she informed me. "I called Staci over Thanksgiving, and she says he'll lend it to me for five dollars."

"Will he rip your bodice off for ten?" I asked.

Giving me a dirty look, Daisy walked right past

the door to the assembly room and continued down the hall. "Hey, I was only joking!" I called after her. "Aren't you coming to assembly?"

"First I have to change," she said.

"You little sneak!" I said. "So that cutesy 'our dress' act was just a bunch of lies!"

Daisy must have felt embarrassed, because she explained that the dress was uncomfortable. "It's tight under the arms. Honest! I must have put on weight since I came here. And the school nurse says I've grown two inches."

I don't believe for a minute that she put on weight, but it's true about growing. Two inches is a lot for four months, but when I asked Gratkins if Daisy had a thyroid problem she said it was just modern nutrition.

"Well, you better hurry," I told Daisy. "You'll get detention if you're late."

Daisy said she'd rather get detention than be seen in her party dress, but she made it back before they closed the doors. Wearing her barf-green gym suit. I'm glad Gratkins wasn't there to see!

Daisy has become hard and calculating. I can barely tolerate her since the evening we went up to the attic. By now, you're supposed to be dying to know what we found up there. The answer is, nothing. That's what's so mind-blowing.

Remember Daisy's last words at the end of chapter nine? She said, "I wonder who I married."

I wondered, too. In fact, we were both so excited that we left the pizza with Laptop and tore upstairs to look in the old albums. But we didn't find a thing. There were plenty of photographs, of course. Family groups, and studio portraits taken at weddings and graduations. There were snapshots of Daisy as she grew older, fifty years ago. We even found one that would do for her interview. But there wasn't a single one of Gratkins with a man.

"Maybe there's another album somewhere," I suggested.

We hunted for ages with no luck. Meanwhile, Daisy grew more and more annoyed. She grumbled, and swore, and started slamming things around. I didn't see why she was so upset. After all, it wasn't as if she could marry the same man that Gratkins did. He's dead now. According to Gratkins, he died a long time ago.

"Listen, who cares?" I told her after a while. "You should be grateful that at least you can choose your own husband. You can marry Staci's brother and be Mrs. Farnham if you like. He'll rip your bodice off three times a day. That beats being plain old Mrs. Atkins!"

Staci Farnham's little brother is only nine. His ears stick out and he picks his nose, so I thought Daisy would get really mad at me. Instead she made a squeaky kind of noise and dropped an old lamp that she was holding.

"But Garet, that's my name already!" she gasped. "Atkins is my *maiden* name, not the name of the guy I marry."

At first she was just confused. She kept trying to

103

work out in her head how she and I and Gratkins could all have the same last name. It didn't do any good for me to point out that lots of women don't change their names when they marry. She just shook her head and said, "She never married. I bet you anything she never married!"

"Then who am I?" I asked finally. "Gratkins must have had children, or she couldn't be my grandmother."

Daisy said that not being married didn't necessarily keep you from having children. "You said so yourself, about my birth certificate," she reminded me. "You said that nowadays, it's classy."

I hate it when people quote things you said before to prove you're wrong now. There ought to be a law against it.

"I don't know what you're getting at," I said, shrugging. "So what if Gratkins didn't have a husband? Why do you have to make such a big deal out of it?"

That's when Daisy's confusion changed to anger. "Because I'm not Gratkins — that's why!" she shouted. "We're not the same person after all. She's lying, and I'm going to prove it."

"How?" I asked.

Daisy's voice softened to a hush. "I'll compare our fingerprints."

What's going to come of it, that's what I want to know. If the fingerprints match up, Daisy will have to face the fact that she's living with her own future. But if they don't, she won't know who she is at all. Which is worse?

Time out for station identification. I'm in the computer room during study hall, and guess who just walked in? Mrs. Magorian and eleven third-graders. I stopped typing to listen for a moment, and I found out they're putting in time on their SWAP project, which happens to be creative similes. Boy, are they ever making a racket! Mrs. Magorian looks more frazzled than usual.

"Remember to speak slowly, girls, because I'm entering your responses on the computer," she said. "Now, what does a sunset bring to mind? Anyone? Anyone?"

A kid with five pink barrettes in her hair said that a sunset was like a squashed tomato.

"Like a squashed road kill, more like," the kid standing next to her said. I recognize that kid: she's Ardeth Shaeffer's little sister.

Mrs. Magorian told Edith Shaeffer to raise her hand next time she had something to share with the class.

"What about a thunderstorm, girls?" she asked, changing the subject.

I knew right away she was in trouble. Kids that age have a lot of imagination, but it all goes into potty talk. I know from personal experience. If you had asked me when I was eight what a thunderstorm was like, I would have gone straight to work on the rumbles and the rain, and even found something gross to compare with lightning. Mrs. Magorian should have known better. She must have realized it herself because she only listened to one answer before changing the subject again.

"And snow, girls?" she asked in the strained voice that in 7-B would have meant someone was about to get detention.

"Snow is like dandruff," Edith Shaeffer said.

Mrs. Magorian sighed and looked out the window. I did, too, and guess what I saw? Snow!

"You're right, Edith," I said. "Someone up in heaven is using the wrong shampoo."

Mrs. Magorian was not amused. She's been lecturing me for the past five minutes on how I'm only allowed in here as long as I don't create a distraction. All the same, she seems thrilled about the snow. So am I. When it snows at Whetstone, they call and tell your parents to pick you up early. It's the first time it ever occurred to me that this could be good news for teachers, too.

Chapter 12

If you ask me, snow is like snow, which happens to be like snow. It's not like dandruff, for sure. Dandruff is dead skin, not crystallized water, and the flakes don't melt when they land on your sweater. They stay there to embarrass you instead. Snow isn't like feathers or a white blanket, either. Both those things are warm and dry.

Why can't Mrs. Magorian leave words alone? Writing would be fun if she'd let me go ahead and say the things I have to say without stopping to put frills on them. If she had her way, my autobiography would end up wearing a peach-colored party dress.

Take yesterday, for instance. The third-graders weren't the only ones who had to play tricks with words. Mrs. Magorian got at us, too, and believe me, it was a lot worse than similes.

"Some of you girls could be more creative in your way of presenting dialogue," she announced in the middle of class. "Perhaps I should say, one of you in particular."

I looked around the room for the culprit, but every

face was blank. Then I looked back at Mrs. Magorian. She was holding one of those manila folders with our printouts from a couple of weeks ago. You guessed right: it was mine.

"Garet Atkins, would you read this passage to the class, please?" she said.

I wrote *said*, not *asked*, on purpose, by the way. In spite of the question mark, this was definitely not a question.

"What happened to 'confidential'?" I objected.

Mrs. Magorian said it wasn't meant to apply to my first five chapters, so I stood up and read that conversation I had with Daisy at the end of chapter three. It was a big hit. The other girls especially liked the part where Daisy explains how learning-disabled kids can get their own computers. But Mrs. Magorian said I had to write it over.

"Now, class," she said. "Has anyone noticed the monotony of Garet's dialogue in this passage?"

The other girls seemed kind of surprised, but I guess they wanted extra credit for giving the right answer, because they all raised their hands.

"How could Garet improve her technique?" Mrs. Magorian asked. "Anyone? Anyone?"

Priscilla Perry raised her hand again. "I think she should leave it out," she said. "It's just a lot of talk, and nothing happens."

I could have killed her. I began to explain that I was setting a mood with that conversation. A suspenseful mood, not a horsey one. But I didn't have to explain anything, because it seems Priscilla gave the wrong answer.

"No, Priscilla," Mrs. Magorian said. "Dialogue actually relieves the monotony in a narrative. But Garet should use verb alternatives for *say*, in order to avoid repetition. Can you girls think of any?"

No one could. "You mean, like *ask?*" I asked.

Mrs. Magorian said that *ask* was every bit as tedious as *say*. According to her, to *quiz* or to *query* would add more color to a question.

"And what are some other ways of expressing verbal interchange?" she quizzed. "Anyone? Anyone?"

At first no one had any ideas. Then Staci Farnham raised her hand. "To breathe throatily," she suggested.

Mrs. Magorian looked puzzled. "I beg your pardon, Staci? Could you give us an example?"

Staci turned kind of red. "Like, 'I have wanted you all my life,' he breathed throatily."

Mrs. Magorian breathed throatily herself, but more as if she wished Staci would dry up. "I see. Anyone else?"

"To whinny," Priscilla whinnied.

Mrs. Magorian didn't ask for more ideas. She just wrote a long list on the blackboard and told us to bear it in mind next time people talk in our autobiographies.

MRS. MAGORIAN'S VERB ALTERNATIVES

beg	bellow	blubber
blurt	chirp	coo
drawl	grin	groan

mumble	murmur	muse
mutter	query	quiz
roar	snort	stammer
yap	yawn	yelp

If you say it fast, this sounds like a crowd scene in a horror movie. I practiced the first four words aloud, because they happen to be real tongue twisters: "Beg, bellow, blubber, blurt. Beg-bellow-blubber-blurt. Begbellowblubberblurt."

Mrs. Magorian got mad. She said I was being disruptive. She also said I had to rewrite my conversation with Daisy right then and there. Here's the new version:

"The kids at school with learning disabilities get extra tutoring, not laptop computers," I mutter.

"That's because they don't play their cards right," Daisy snorts.

"I wouldn't want to risk it. I bet you wouldn't either," I chirp.

"I would so," she blubbers.

"You would not," I yelp.

"How much do you want to bet?" she queries.

"I'll bet a million dollars," I coo.

"You don't have a million dollars," she yawns.

"Then I'll bet anything you like," I yap.

"You don't *have* anything I like," she bellows, "so I guess I won't bet after all."

"Chicken!" I grin.

I like my original version better, but anything to get an A in English! I have a problem with some of the verbs on Mrs. Magorian's list, though. It's not easy to yawn a whole sentence. In some cases, it's impossible to yawn even a single word. "Chicken," for example. But it's possible to *grin* "chicken." I tried it.

I made Daisy try on the way home in that snowstorm yesterday. We were in the backseat, sitting on a plastic bag put there by Gratkins. This is because yesterday was the annual soccer game between Whetstone Academy and the girls' team from Whetstone Junior High. The Junior High team had already arrived when it started snowing, so we played anyway and got mashed. We always get mashed. The town kids don't have to try. They don't even lose their breath, so they have plenty left to make personal remarks about our barf-green gym suits with name tapes on the pockets. But we don't always get so wet, which is why the plastic bag.

I happen to be good at soccer. Not Daisy. She isn't the athletic type, which made it all the more infuriating that by accident she scored the only goal. This meant everybody hugged her and that kind of thing. She ought to have been happy. Instead, she sat there shivering and looking really blue. Considering the unfairness of that accidental goal, I think it was nice of me to cheer her up.

"Chicken!" I grinned.

Daisy swiveled her head around like an owl and stared at me without cracking a smile.

"Didn't Daisy score the only goal?" Gratkins asked from the front seat. "I do believe you're jealous!"

"I was trying to cheer her up," I protested. Then I explained about Mrs. Magorian's list of alternative verbs.

"Some of it works fine," I told her. "For instance, you can grin 'chicken,' and you can groan it, but if you try to stammer 'chicken,' it comes out sounding like a sneeze."

Daisy kept on staring at me in her owly way. She took a deep breath and tried to stammer "chicken." I was right: it sounded like a sneeze.

"See what I mean?" I said. "Okay, I'll give you two more of Mrs. Magorian's words. You can bellow 'chicken,' but have you ever tried to beg it?"

"Beg it for what?" Gratkins asked.

"Just try it," I said. "It's fun!"

Daisy cleared her throat a couple of times. "Chicken," she said. Just said. Her heart obviously wasn't in it. Neither was her mind, because the next thing she said was, "Why didn't you ever get married, Gratkins?"

Gratkins was quiet for a long time, during which she kind of over-drove. Meaning she signaled more than necessary and kept putting her brake on. Then she'd speed up again and check the rearview mirror even though we were the only car on the road. The snow was coming down fast and thick by then. Huge, wet swirls of it slapped against the windshield. I was scared we'd have an accident.

"You didn't answer my question," Daisy remarked coolly. "Would that be for any particular reason?"

In this really fakey voice, Gratkins started talking about "The Young and the Restless." "I'm so worried about those young people," she told Daisy. "How can Ashley and Brad work things out if they won't communicate? I'm afraid something awful will happen in tomorrow's episode!"

"It's today's episode I'm worried about," said Daisy. "And guess what? It's taking place in the privacy of our own home, not on a TV screen. What is the sordid secret of this woman's life?"

I laughed nervously. Gratkins skidded into our driveway and practically fell out of the car, she was in such a hurry opening the door. Daisy actually did fall. She was in a hurry, too, so she tripped over Laptop, who always skitters in circles when we get home from school. But she picked herself up and ran after Gratkins, catching up at the front door.

"What are you trying to hide?" she asked angrily. "Why did you pretend to be married when you weren't?"

Gratkins sighed and paused for a moment before she turned the knob. "I have a roast in the oven," she said. "I can't talk now."

I changed into dry clothes and went to the kitchen to see if I could help. I wasn't surprised to find Gratkins on a stool at the counter, watching "Oprah" on the little TV she has in there. What surprised me was that the kitchen didn't smell of roast. I looked in the oven to make sure, but it was cold and empty. Imagine Gratkins telling a fib like that! Maybe she hasn't changed much since she was Daisy's age.

"Don't let it burn," I said.

Gratkins gave a little start and looked up from the screen. "I'll put it in the minute the show is over," she promised guiltily.

"What's going on?" I demanded. "Something really weird is going on in this house, and I don't like it. I don't blame Daisy for pestering you."

"Wait for the commercial," said Gratkins.

Somehow I doubted that Daisy would wait for any commercial, either on TV or in real life. Not in the mood she was in. She wanted an answer from Gratkins, and she was going to play her cards right until she got it. Where *was* Daisy, by the way? I went to her room and found her still shivering in her wet gym suit.

"You'll catch your death!" I said.

Daisy sneezed and unbuttoned the top button. "If I do, will Gratkins die, too? Or does Gratkins have to die first, in which case I can do anything I like as long as she stays healthy?"

"I thought you'd decided you weren't the same person," I reminded her.

"Isn't that obvious from the way she's been lying to me?" Daisy pulled the detective kit out of her book bag. "We'll find out soon enough, though. You read the instructions while I get dressed."

I would rather have gone outside in the snow, but by this time it had turned to drizzle. "Too bad there

114

wasn't a real blizzard," I said, opening the kit. "Hey, this is neat! Can I try?"

"Be my guest." Daisy yanked a comb through the tangles in her ponytail.

Taking your fingerprints is fun. You get to smush your fingers around on an ink pad and then press them on a sheet of paper. I did all eight fingers and both thumbs. It was interesting to see how my left and right hand varied a little, and how the pattern was broken by the scar where I cut myself slicing a lemon last summer. It was a decorative pattern, in an artsy way.

"Can I keep these?" I asked.

Daisy shrugged. "What for?"

"Wallpaper. I'll print up a whole bunch of copies, and paste them on my wall. It'll look fantastic!"

"Be my guest," Daisy said again.

By the time I came back from my room, Daisy had changed into jeans. I followed her to the kitchen, which finally smelled of roast. Gratkins had found time to put it in the oven during a commercial, but she was still glued to the screen. In fact, she wouldn't speak to us until the show was over.

"You girls should have watched from the beginning," she said as she switched the power off. "Oprah has been interviewing a woman who writes horoscopes, and guess what?"

"Who cares?" Daisy asked.

It was obvious that Gratkins felt snubbed, although she tried to brush it off by remarking that horoscopes were always good for a laugh. "I'm sure you think I'm just a silly old woman," she added breezily. If you ask me, it was a chilly breeze.

This was Daisy's cue to say something reassuring, such as that Gratkins wasn't old and silly. But did Daisy pick up the cue? Dream on! Daisy fiddled with her ponytail and looked bored the whole time Gratkins was talking. I could tell she was *trying* to look bored. "Can we do our fingerprints now?" she asked.

Gratkins didn't bother to answer. Instead she held out her hand and let Daisy press her fingers on the ink pad, followed by a sheet of paper. When Daisy had finished with Gratkins, she repeated the process with her own fingers. I watched anxiously as she inspected the results. The suspense was killing me.

The suspense should be killing The Intelligent Reader, too. Does Daisy shout for joy? Does Daisy shriek with rage? Surprise, surprise — Daisy doesn't do either! Daisy drops the sheet of paper into the trash.

A puzzled frown creased Gratkins's face. "What's the matter, honey? Didn't they come out right?"

Daisy's voice was colder than ever. "I guess that depends on what you mean by 'right.' If 'right' means I grow up to be a silly old woman who pretends she had a husband when she didn't, then it came out right. If you happen to be someone who'd rather die than grow up that way, then it came out wrong. But don't let it bother you."

Someday soon I may kill Daisy. How could anyone deliberately hurt a person as nice as Gratkins? Besides, she should know that by hurting Gratkins, she's only hurting her future self.

116

"You're a rat, Daisy!" I said. It sounded feeble, so I phrased it differently. "You're a scumball, Daisy. I'm sorry people think you're my sister."

Daisy blew her nose into a paper towel, scowled at the towel, and threw it at Laptop, who crawled into the space under the sink.

When no one was looking, I fished the fingerprint paper out of the trash again and put it with the others in my bottom bureau drawer. As soon as this fuss has blown over, I'll go ahead with my decorating plans. Maybe I'll dye my blankets black, and have only white cases on my pillows. It would make a welcome change from Daisy's flowery, flouncy canopy bed.

Speaking of Daisy, she went straight to her room and hasn't left it since. I'm not kidding! She didn't come out to eat the roast, or say good night or anything. You'd think she'd at least come out to use the toilet, but if she did, I didn't see her. And she didn't come to school today. Why not? Because she's sick, or so she says. According to Daisy, when she sneezed "chicken," it was the start of a cold.

Chapter 13

Is she sick or isn't she? That's what I want to know. I snuck into Daisy's room before I left for school this morning and asked if it was a real cold. By way of answering, she blew her nose. I wasn't convinced. Gratkins lets her get away with murder!

"Are you coming to school tomorrow?" I asked.

"Not if I play my cards right," said Daisy.

If that meant dressing the part, there was no doubt she was playing her cards right. Remember Daisy's notebook with lists of what to wear when? There's a list for being sick in bed. It goes from her head (#1: Mussed-up hair, tied back with ribbon) to her feet (#7: Shell-pink toenail polish), and includes things that don't belong to her (#4: Borrow Garet's Earth Day T-shirt). How calculating can a person get? Plus *borrow* is hardly the word for how she got my T-shirt. She never asked. As for her hair, I bet she set the alarm for six to get that mussed-up effect. I hope it hurts when she tries to comb it out.

On the other hand, there were signs that all was

not right with Daisy. Dark smudges under her eyes, for one thing, and for another thing her nose. When she blew it again, I took a good look. It was shiny, red, and runny. Daisy cares too much about her appearance to fake a shiny, red, runny nose.

"Well, what do you know!" I said.

"I know how to play my cards right," said Daisy.

Maybe she does and maybe she doesn't. What *I* know is that she missed a great assembly. When I walked into school today there were posters up all over the place saying things like "What's Your Education Worth? SWAP and Find Out!" There was also a big banner over the double doors to the assembly hall. It said, WELCOME LEON PRINER!

"Who's Leon Priner?" I asked the girl next to me.

She was an eighth-grader, so I had to put up with the usual how-dumb-can-you-get stare before she honored me with an answer. Namely that Leon Priner was the author who had been invited to give out prizes at the end of SWAP.

"The end?" I said. "You're kidding! 7-B hasn't finished its autobiographies yet."

She raised her eyebrows, as much as to say, "Wow, this one is dumber than most!" and told me that 7-B never finished anything. Not that it mattered, because everyone knew that the eighth-graders would clean up all the prizes.

So SWAP was over. I had a sinking feeling that this meant trouble, and I was right. But I'll tell about the trouble after I tell about Leon Priner, who was already on stage in a rocking chair. He was a white-haired, bony kind of man who looked about as comfortable in that rocker as a baby on a bar stool. He grinned at us, but his eyes weren't with it. He kept nervously reaching his hand up to a bulge in his shirt pocket that I guessed was a pack of cigarettes. Each time he reached, he glanced at the NO SMOK-ING signs and drew his hand away again. I felt sorry for the man.

"Why the rocker?" I asked the eighth-grader.

She looked at me pityingly. "Leon Priner writes stories for kids, dummy. Kids' authors always sit in rockers."

I was interested to find out if they had any choice in the matter, and if they typed their stories sitting in a rocker, too. It didn't sound like an easy way to work.

"Shut up!" she said. "They're starting the flag salute."

Hardly anyone joined in the flag salute this morning. We were all too busy staring. It's not often we get a guest speaker at Whetstone. When we do, it's never a male. The headmistress hopes we won't find out that males exist until we graduate. That's one reason why we don't have any male teachers. The other reason is Staci Farnham. This Leon Priner was a little old for us, but undeniably male.

After the flag salute, the headmistress said we were fortunate in having the author of *With a Bang AND a Whimper* as a guest speaker and that Mrs. Magorian would introduce him. Then she sat down in a hurry, as if she were glad to get out of introducing him herself. I bet she hasn't read his book. I haven't either. I've never even heard of Leon Priner.

"Do *you* know who this guy is?" I asked.

"Shut up!" the eighth-grader hissed. "Mrs. Magorian is going to speak."

Mrs. Magorian not only knew who Leon Priner was, she had also read his book. She said a whole bunch of gushy things like, "It was so exciting, I couldn't put it down!" and, "Aren't we lucky, girls? A real, live professional author here at Whetstone Academy!" She went on for so long that Leon Priner yawned. I think Mrs. Magorian noticed because she quit gushing and went back to her seat.

Everybody clapped, and then we all settled down to watch the clock. Most of the guest speakers at Whetstone are pretty boring, so all we care about is whether we get to skip our first class. Leon Priner was different. He started out cracking a few lame jokes, but as soon as he switched from what was supposed to interest us (the beginning of a young writer) to what actually interested *him* (the end of the world), things began to pick up.

First he explained that he wrote science fiction. Then he explained why: it's because he's concerned about the future of the planet Earth. From there he went into what that future would be like (short), who was responsible for it (us), and what we could do about it (things that are against the rules at Whetstone).

We all stopped looking at the clock and began listening instead. Unfortunately, so did the faculty. And when Priner got to the part about going on a hunger strike if the Academy cafeteria continued using disposable Styrofoam containers, the headmistress interrupted him. "Now, girls," she said, "I'm sure

Mr. Priner wants to get back to his typewriter, so how do we show our appreciation?"

Everybody clapped again, but Mrs. Magorian wasn't about to let us off that easily. "Questions?" she suggested. "Anyone? Anyone?"

There was a long silence, during which we all tried to look invisible. But Mrs. Magorian gave us the evil eye, so I raised my hand and asked why Leon Priner smoked cigarettes if he was so big on not polluting the environment.

Mrs. Magorian didn't even give him time to answer. She just pointed at another hand that had gone up and said, "Next question, please?"

The next question was, "Are you *The* Professional Author?" I could tell from the whinny that it had been asked by Priscilla Perry.

Leon Priner crossed his legs, making the rocker heave so that it nearly tipped him over. I'm afraid we giggled.

"I beg your pardon?" he said.

Priscilla repeated her question but he still didn't catch on. "Which professional author did you have in mind?" he asked.

Priscilla tossed her mane at Mrs. Magorian. "You never told us there were *two!*" she whinnied.

Leon Priner looked around the assembly hall as if he were checking out the emergency exits, so Mrs. Magorian stood up and started gushing again. She said how *With a Bang AND a Whimper* was a breathtaking achievement of the literary year, and asked how he managed to create such a chilling aura of suspense.

"The end of the world provides its own chilling aura of suspense," said Leon Priner. "As an author, I felt obliged to write about it."

Personally, I think he was in a hurry to leave. In fact, I know he was, because he got halfway to the door before Mrs. Magorian reminded him that he was supposed to give out prizes. So he came back and presented the blue ribbon to a kid in 5-B for her story about a turkey that ran for president. The eighth-grader sitting next to me got an honorable mention, which came wrapped in silver paper. I hope it's chocolates and she chokes on them.

As I said, it was a great assembly, only I wish I'd thought to ask Leon Priner for some useful tips. When does an autobiography stop being an autobiography and start being a journal, for example? Mrs. Magorian says we ought to know. She said so as soon as we walked into English class. She was in a no-nonsense mood, and it went like this:

Mrs. M.: "All right, girls. Please give your autobiographies a final check and be prepared to print them out tomorrow."

7-B: [howls of rage and disbelief]

Mrs. M.: "Now, girls! It's high time we all stopped trying to be writers and got back to real life."

Priscilla: "But I haven't won the Kentucky Derby yet!"

Staci: "And I haven't married my duke!"

123

Mrs. M.: "Don't you girls know the difference between an autobiography and
an ongoing journal?"

It sounds to me as if Mrs. Magorian doesn't know
the difference between fact and fiction. Staci won't
even get a blind date with a love-crazed duke until
she's out of braces. And if Priscilla doesn't lose twenty
pounds, there's no way she can win the Kentucky
Derby. At least not unless she enters as the horse.
But Mrs. Magorian raves about every word they write,
while she acts as if I were trying to put something
over on her. When I left class this morning, for instance, she told me to step aside.

"How are you coming along with your little story,
Garet?" she inquired in the sweetly concerned voice
most people use to ask for news of someone they
don't like but who is terminally ill. Notice that she
said "story," not "autobiography"!

I answered that the story *of my life* was coming on
as well as could be expected for a life like mine.
"Give me another week or so and I'll find a good place
to end it," I suggested. "End my story, not my life,
that is."

Mrs. Magorian said she was sorry, but we were
about to begin another project. "However, I'll make
an exception for you, Garet," she added as if she were
doing me a huge favor. "There aren't enough printers
for everyone to print out their diskettes at once. I'll
put your name at the end of the list. That will give
you until Friday."

Big deal! Today is already Wednesday. I came in

during study hall to write this chapter, but the bell is about to ring, which means I have to stop writing and go to sports. Besides, what can possibly happen between now and Friday that will turn my autobiography into a breathtaking achievement of the literary year? Nothing — that's what. So why don't you take your pick of endings and finish it yourself?

CHOOSE YOUR OWN ENDING

1. Mrs. Magorian elopes with Leon Priner. Garet Atkins writes the story of *their* lives and wins the Pulitzer Prize for her breathtaking achievement of the literary year. The girls in 7-B get an open-minded substitute.
2. The police raid the Whetstone Academy cafeteria and discover a stash of festering road kill. The cafeteria is closed for the remainder of the school year. Meanwhile, McDonald's caters us at noon.
3. Schoolwide intelligence testing reveals that Garet Atkins is smarter than Daisy Atkins. Garet gets moved up to 7-A. Daisy gets moved down to 6-B. Mrs. Magorian offers a formal apology to Garet, who accepts.
4. Daisy disappears off the face of the earth.

Chapter 14

You're never going to believe it, but that's precisely what Daisy did. Ending number four wins, ladies and gents: Ms. Daisy Atkins disappears off the face of the planet Earth!

Seriously, Daisy is gone. Today is Thursday, and I figure she left the house about the same time I left for school this morning, because Gratkins didn't see her when she got back from driving me. Not that she looked, at first. She assumed that Daisy was still asleep, so she left her alone until it was time for "As the World Turns." When she went to get her, she found this note on Daisy's pillow:

> *Dear Gratkins,*
> *I'm sorry, but I can't live with you anymore. Please don't try to find me, and please don't get mad. I love you, but I'd rather be myself.*
> *Tell Garet she can sleep in my canopy bed and have my computer.*
>
> *Love,*
> *Daisy*

In a pathetic way it's funny. I mean, usually when a kid runs away from home you call the police. But how do you report a missing kid when you can't explain where that kid came from in the first place? The people at Whetstone Academy swallowed our long-lost twin story, but Gratkins says detectives are smarter. I'm afraid she's right.

"I'm glad Daisy is gone!" I told her when she picked me up at school this afternoon. "You should be glad, too. She's been nothing but trouble."

The reason I said this was that Gratkins had been crying, and it made me mad. Would she cry as much for me if I ran away from home? Dream on! She keeps asking what she could have done to make Daisy stay. My answer is that I don't know. Probably nothing except be a different kind of old lady, but I can't say that. Finally I took Daisy's laptop into my room so I could write down what happened.

According to Daisy, it's my laptop now. She left it at a convenient time, because now I can continue my autobiography. I should feel thrilled, but it doesn't seem right to use it. I doubt I'll be able to sleep in Daisy's canopy bed either. Why did she run off like that? Didn't she know how badly Gratkins would miss her? It wasn't my fault, anyway. I warned Gratkins that something was really wrong. And I didn't mean Daisy's so-called cold. I meant the weird way she's been acting lately.

Take last night, for instance. I did my homework in Daisy's room, to keep her company. She had homework, too. Piles of homework. But she wasn't doing it. She just sat on her canopy bed with the quilt over her shoulders, even though it wasn't cold. She was still wearing the sick-in-bed outfit, which smelled ready for the wash. She got on my nerves. But what really got on my nerves was Laptop. He lay curled up on the bed as if he were her dog instead of mine.

"What's an object complement?" I asked.

"Search me," said Daisy.

"I thought 7-A did this chapter last week," I said, holding up the grammar textbook. "In fact, I know you did."

"Well, I've forgotten then."

I groaned and took a closer look at her. There was a haunted expression on her face. Haunted and also kind of scared. She looked skinnier than usual, too. I don't know how two days at home with a cold can make a person lose weight. When I find out, I'll give it a try.

"You look terrible!" I said. "Not just sick-terrible. Depressed-terrible, too. What have you been doing all day?"

Daisy said she'd been watching the soaps. I was sorry I asked, because she started telling me all the plots.

"Jack met his parole officer again today," she informed me. "Ashley's acting really weird. I wonder if she's going to make it up with Brad?"

I tried to seem interested. I've never been hooked on the soaps, but some of my friends in 7-B are, so I'm familiar with the characters. That's how I noticed when Daisy began to mix them up.

"You know what?" she said after she had babbled

on for a while. "I think Frisco is the father of Mollie's baby."

I was diagramming sentences, which is hard enough in what Mrs. Magorian calls "a work-conducive atmosphere." Daisy's whacky comment totally blew my concentration.

"Let me get this straight," I said, closing the textbook. "Mollie is out of 'The Young and the Restless,' right?"

Daisy nodded eagerly. "She doesn't want to tell the welfare worker who the father is, and —"

"That's not the point," I said, interrupting her. "Isn't Frisco out of 'General Hospital'?"

Daisy nodded again and gave me a wide-eyed, spacey look. I noticed that the smudges under her eyes were growing smudgier.

"So how did Frisco get Mollie pregnant?" I asked. "It takes a minimal amount of body contact, you know."

I thought she'd correct her mistake. Instead she explained how Mollie and Frisco met at Delila's house. Now, I happen to know that Delila is out of "One Life to Live." I wasn't about to argue though, because we had a quiz in the morning. If you don't pass your grammar quizzes, Mrs. Magorian makes you take them again during study hall. I needed my study hall for some tricky editing on my autobiography. First I wanted to print a full-length version for myself. Then I planned to cut a lot of stuff out and make a short-and-sweet version for Mrs. Magorian.

"Are you coming to school tomorrow?" I asked Daisy.

She gave me a reproachful look. "I can't. I'm sick."

"Sicker people than you come to school," I said. "You're going to fall behind. Why don't you come anyway?"

"I can't," she repeated.

"It's just you're too lazy to make up your homework," I told her scornfully. "I have to do mine, all the same. Either you quit babbling or I'm moving to someplace quiet."

She kept on babbling, so I packed up my books and left. I didn't go straight to my room, though. I went to find Gratkins first. She was where she usually is at that time of evening: sitting on a stool at the kitchen counter, eating mints and reading her horoscope. When I walked in, she offered me the bowl of mints but didn't look up.

"Listen to this, Daisy. It says here that Scorpios should put romance on hold."

"I'm Garet," I told her. "How about putting your horoscope on hold for a minute? I'm worried about Daisy."

That got her attention. She lowered the paper and stared innocently at me. "Daisy? Why on earth would you worry about Daisy? Her cold is getting better."

"Are you sure it's only a cold?" I asked. "Isn't there something called brain fever?"

Gratkins said if there was, Daisy would be the last person to have it. "She's so smart!" she boasted. "It's hard to believe I was so smart at her age. Why, take this afternoon. We were watching 'One Life to Live,' and Rafe had just been telling Delila how she needs a purpose in her life — something to live for, right? Well, during the last commercial, Daisy said Delila ought to start a home for unwed mothers. You'll never in a million years guess why!"

"So Mollie can stay there while she waits to have her baby?" I suggested.

Gratkins beamed. "Now, admit it. Wasn't that a brilliant idea?"

"There's just one problem," I told her, trying to keep my voice calm and patient. "Mollie's not in 'One Life to Live.' Mollie's in 'The Young and the Restless.' "

"That's why it's such a good idea," Gratkins said triumphantly. "If she has her baby on another soap, it won't cause so much talk."

Daisy shouldn't worry about growing up to be like Gratkins. She already *is* like Gratkins. That's why she should have stayed. At least they understand each other! But I guess it's no use saying "should," because she's gone.

By the way, it's not true that I'm glad she's gone. I want her to come back.

Chapter 15

Today is Friday. Daisy has been gone for a day and a half already. The house seems really weird without her. Not just because Gratkins is moping around. Or because Laptop sits on the canopy bed and whines. But also because of me. I miss Daisy. I worry about her, too.

It's late at night now, and I'm tired. This has been a terrible day! But I wanted to write down what happened, and to do that, I had to wait for the power to come back on. Why did the power go off? We had a storm — that's why. But not until the end of the day. I'll start at the beginning.

I did some detective work this morning at school. People were beginning to ask about Daisy, since it's unusual to stay out four days for a cold. I told the teachers that she was really sick, but I hinted to the kids that she was faking. I figured they'd tell me if they'd seen her hanging around the shopping mall, but no one had. Of course, our local mall is tiny. Maybe Daisy ran away to a mega-mall, like the ones closer to the city. What an airhead! Does she think the world out there is safe, like sitcoms on TV? Doesn't she realize that I have to account for her?

"Tell your grandmother that I'll need a doctor's note if Daisy stays out any longer," the headmistress said when she passed me in the hall.

That's all Gratkins needs is to forge a medical excuse. I was already in a bad mood when I walked into English class and handed over the short-and-sweet version of my autobiography. The mood got worse when I found out too late that since we missed the Leon Priner deadline, Mrs. Magorian was going to give her own prize for the best autobiography. If I had known, I would have spiced mine up a bit! With lies like Staci's, of course. Not with the true parts that for safety's sake, I had to edit.

Editing hadn't been an easy job. It meant going way back to chapter six to take out the parts that might make people suspicious. It was embarrassing to read how often I complained about Daisy. I felt like a creep. My only consolation was knowing how pleased Mrs. Magorian would be that I'd been able to print it out yesterday after all. But she didn't look at it. She just dropped it into one of her desk drawers and told me to sit down because she was about to make an announcement.

"It's a very *exciting* announcement," she informed the class. "Whetstone Academy has been invited to participate in a nationwide writing contest!"

We were all quiet, and I didn't sense much enthusiasm. Mrs. Magorian kept right on raving all the same.

"Now, I know you're dying to learn more about this," she said, beaming at us, "so I'll give you each a copy of the entry rules. The theme of the contest is 'Earth, Our Garden' and we want to send in a set of essays that Whetstone can be proud of. Don't we, girls?"

I raised my hand. "Would it be okay if we went on with our autobiographies instead?"

Mrs. Magorian gave me a weary look. "I thought I had already made that clear, Garet. The SWAP project is over. As of today, we'll stop writing about ourselves and start writing about this planet that we live on."

"That's kind of silly, isn't it?" I asked.

She raised her eyebrows. "I beg your pardon, Garet?"

I knew I'd get into trouble, but I was upset about Daisy so I didn't have the sense to shut up. "It's silly," I repeated. "I mean, I take it we're supposed to write about the flora and fauna of our planet. Right?"

"I imagine so, but I'd have to look at the rules," she answered warily.

"If Earth is our garden, then things like seaweed and turnips and skunk cabbage all grow in it," I pointed out.

Mrs. Magorian nodded. "That's very true, Garet."

"And ducks and mosquitoes and gerbils," I continued. "They grow in Earth's garden, too, don't they?"

The other girls started to giggle, so I finished up fast, before anyone could change the subject. "What

134

about people, then? How can you say we're not part of Earth, Our Garden?"

"I never said we weren't," Mrs. Magorian answered coldly. "I only said it was time to stop working on your autobiography."

"Well, that's what's silly!" I told her. "If I were a gerbil, you wouldn't be telling me to stop working on my autobiography. Do I have to grow fur to rate?"

"Garet, that will do!" she snapped. "You'll stay after school for detention this afternoon. In the teachers' lounge, not the computer room. I'll expect you there at three o'clock."

The teachers' lounge is the most dismal place you can imagine. To begin with, there's a strong smell of coffee that's been brewing since dawn. It comes from a tray in the corner with a bunch of Styrofoam cups on it, and Coffee-Mate, and packets of artificial sweetener. Grim! Then there's a permanent smell of stale tobacco. I happen to know that the Health and Hygiene teacher used to smoke in there, but this fall the other teachers ganged up on her and said she had to go outdoors. The smell stuck to the armchairs, which are Danish modern left over from the fifties, upholstered in barf-green Naugahyde with scum imbedded in the cracks. If I were a teacher, I'd hold out for real furniture, even if it's from a yard sale. And I'd put pictures on the wall. The teachers' lounge at Whetstone just has announcements.

I stood and read the announcements for a while. They were all for things like tutoring schedules and deadlines for midterm grades and flyers about weekend seminars for educators. I read the flyers carefully to see if they ever used the word *teacher*. They never did. I was daydreaming about how it would be if *teacher* became a dirty word when Mrs. Magorian walked in.

"Good afternoon, Garet," she said.

The greeting slid through her tight, thin lips as if she were sliding a dime into a parking meter. Then she lectured me on keeping things within proportion. Meaning I should learn not to go too far. The main thing I've been going too far with, according to Mrs. Magorian, is my autobiography.

"I meant it to be a convenient vehicle of self-expression, through which you girls could practice your structural and stylistic skills," she explained. "I didn't mean it to become an obsession."

Maybe Mrs. Magorian has a dictionary programmed into her, like Daisy's laptop. "Obsession?" I repeated.

"Obsession," she said firmly. "The other teachers tell me you've been neglecting your work. Taking notes for your autobiography during class. That sort of thing."

"Notes?" I repeated. "Who says I'm taking notes?"

Talk of unfair! It's true that I jot down a word from time to time, but you can hardly call it taking notes. It's just so I don't forget something important next time I'm at the computer.

"My grades haven't gone down," I argued.

"From what I hear, your grades *couldn't* go down, except in math."

She had backed me into a corner. "Okay, so my

grades are a problem," I admitted. "That's why I need to verbalize my antagonisms by writing about them in my autobiography."

Mrs. Magorian gave me a suspicious look. Then she softened a little and almost smiled. "I'm glad you enjoy writing, Garet. It's an obsession that I share, believe it or not. But you have to train yourself to diversify."

"Diversify?" I repeated. I felt pretty stupid, echoing back what she said, but I couldn't help it. I was getting that mouse-with-a-snake feeling again.

Mrs. Magorian poured herself a cup of foul-smelling coffee. "This new project will make a nice change for you," she said, stirring in Coffee-Mate and NutraSweet. "It will take you out of yourself. I called your grandmother and asked her to pick you up an hour late. I'd like you to use the time to plan your essay on 'Earth, Our Garden.' "

I couldn't think of anything else to do for an hour, so I took her advice. Except for one thing: I hate essays. If I write anything, I'll write a story. It's going to be about a country called New Pork where the people are all carnarians. Meaning meat eaters, as opposed to vegetarians. In this country it's okay to eat meat, but eating vegetables is a crime. If you get caught, you go to jail for it. My heroine is called Marian the Carnarian. She hates road kill, which is all her mother ever serves her. At the end she gets put in jail for pulling a turnip out of Earth, Our Garden.

I wrote for about forty minutes. At first it was fun, but then I got this terrible cramp in my arm. Writing longhand is something I hardly ever do. I knew I'd go much faster on a computer, and I was really mad at Mrs. Magorian for making me do detention in a place where I couldn't use one. So I quit writing and looked out the window instead.

All the school buses had gone, but a bunch of girls were hanging out on the front steps, waiting to be picked up. Their hair and skirts were blowing around like crazy, which is how I first noticed the wind. I adore wind, so I opened the window and leaned way out.

It was eerie weather: wild and damp. The last of the yellow leaves swirled into the sky, and the leaves that had already fallen gave off a sour, woodsy smell. The sky was dark gray, but the trees and houses seemed bright anyway, as if the sun were shining on them from hidden places. It was no afternoon to stay late in detention. I was relieved when I saw our car turning the corner at the far end of the street. Grabbing my backpack, I ran outside feeling high and happy. I had this weird premonition that something good was about to happen. I thought I knew what it was.

"Daisy's home!" I shouted as I tumbled into the car. "She came home, didn't she?"

But Gratkins shook her head.

"Then she's coming," I assured her. Or maybe I was only assuring myself, because I couldn't believe my premonition had been wrong. "She changed her mind, and when we get home she'll be there."

Gratkins drove several blocks before she said a word. When she finally spoke, her voice trembled:

"She's not coming home, Garet, honey. She's gone back to her own time."

Me with my brilliant ideas about mega-malls — how could I have been so dumb? I should have known Daisy would put on that peach-colored party dress and climb back up the laundry chute.

Chapter 16

"But how did she do it?" I asked. "How did you find out?"

It seems it was Laptop who found out. Gratkins was looking for him to take him for his walk, and found him in Daisy's room. She picked up the room a bit while she was there, which is how she happened to notice that the peach-colored dress was gone. She also noticed that Daisy's bed was all messed up from when she had a cold, so she put the sheets in the washer and went to get a clean pair from the linen closet in the upstairs hall. Laptop followed her.

"And oh, Garet!" Gratkins added shakily. "You should have seen how he carried on when he was there. Yelping, and scratching at that little flap to the laundry chute that your great-grandfather nailed up long ago! Then I noticed that it wasn't nailed up anymore. Someone had opened it again, and there was a rope dangling down it, of all things."

"A rope?" I repeated. "Why a rope? Why didn't she just slide down, the way she did before?"

"Because she climbed up instead," said Gratkins. "It makes sense, doesn't it? If sliding down brought her to the future, then climbing back up took her to the past. Daisy is smart. She'd have no trouble figuring it out."

She may be smart, but she's not athletic. Hauling herself up that chute would be hard enough in a barf-green gym suit. In a frilly dress, it would be nearly impossible.

When I told Gratkins this, she said that Daisy had no choice. "She had to go home wearing what she wore when she left," she explained. "You see, I think she's hoping to be reabsorbed. If she's exactly the same as the Margaret she used to be, the two might merge together."

A little knot of ache tightened in my throat. Did that mean Daisy was gone forever? That she had chosen her parents over Gratkins, and some long-ago sister over me? I had a feeling I was going to cry. But tears were the last thing Gratkins needed, so I changed the subject.

"What happened on 'The Young and the Restless' today? Did Mollie have her baby yet?"

Gratkins said she hadn't had the heart to watch. I tried to think of something else to talk about, but my thoughts kept going back to Daisy. What happened once she climbed up to 1943? How had it felt to merge into the Daisy that she had separated from?

"I wonder if she was scared," I said aloud.

"Scared?" Gratkins repeated.

"To go back to the past," I explained. "I would have been! Don't you remember anything about it?

Like feeling part of yourself kind of disappear one day when you were twelve years old, and then come back again when you were thirteen?"

"Not a thing," she said. "I led a perfectly normal life."

"Except you were cloned," I reminded her.

Gratkins shook her head. "Cloning is scientific. Something to do with cells — I read about it in the paper. What happened to Daisy was magic. Not everyone notices when something magic happens."

"*I* would," I said.

She gave me a funny look. "Would you? Well, I didn't."

"Maybe you weren't the noticing type," I said. "It's lucky your parents nailed up the flap. Otherwise it might have happened again. Just think if there were hundreds of Margarets popping out of that chute. Where would we put them all?"

Gratkins gave me another funny look, but she didn't answer. And I didn't try to talk anymore, because by that time we could hear the wind howling even with the car windows shut. When we got home, a couple of big branches had fallen on our front lawn, and Gratkins began to fuss about the roof.

"That's all we need to start the winter," she said gloomily. "Holes in the roof! Roofing costs an arm and a leg these days, but then plastering does, too. If I let the roof go, the water will leak down through the attic and next thing we know, the ceilings will start to flake. I don't know where you expect me to find the money!"

I couldn't help laughing. "I don't expect anything, Gratkins. Nothing's fallen on the roof yet, anyway."

Gratkins said how did I know those branches on the lawn hadn't hit the roof first. I told her I knew because there weren't any shingles on the lawn. But she said that didn't prove anything, and I should go up to the attic to look for leaks.

"There won't be any," I said. "It isn't raining."

"If it isn't yet, it will be soon," she prophesied.

She was right. There was a flash of lightning, followed a few seconds later by thunder. The sky grew darker than ever, and rain came pelting down.

"See?" Gratkins said triumphantly. "Now we're in for it! Take a flashlight in case the power goes off. And get some pots out of the kitchen for the leaks."

I figured it would be better to go than to stay there arguing, so I headed for the kitchen. I wasn't out of the room before she called me back, however. And "called" is putting it mildly. It sounded more like a wail.

"What's the matter?" I asked.

Her face had turned pale, and there were tears in her eyes again. "What if I'm wrong?" she asked. "What if the rope was just a trick to put us off her trail?"

"That would be good," I told her. "That would mean she's still around."

The tears spilled over and trickled down Gratkins's cheeks, leaving wobbly paths in her face powder. "Maybe she's out in the storm. Go look for her, Garet. The leaks can wait."

I don't know what happened to me then. Jealousy,

I guess, because goodness knows I wanted Daisy back, too. But anger welled up in me like vomit, and I had to spit it out.

"Do you realize what you said?" I asked. "Do you have any *idea* what you just said? You don't want Daisy out in the storm, so I should go out in the storm to look for her! Don't you care if I get struck by lightning? Or do I have to come out of the past, too, to make you care?"

Gratkins caught her breath and sort of stumbled backward. "Why, Garet! I just meant —"

"You meant that you love Daisy more than you love me!" I interrupted. My cheeks burned and my ears throbbed as all my stored-up gripes came jostling out. "It's no use lying about it. You've made it perfectly clear ever since she came here. You think she's prettier and smarter, and you're right. But it's not fair!"

Gratkins started breathing normally again and moved in my direction. "Honey, you couldn't be more wrong! If I seemed to favor Daisy, it's only because I felt sorry that she never had the advantages I've been able to give *you*. I've been loving you since you were two years old, remember? Daisy had a lot of catching up to do."

She must have run out of steam at this point, because she stopped and stared at me for a while. I stared back, scowling. I wasn't going to let her sweet-talk me out of this one.

"Garet, I love you just as much as Daisy," she said softly. "I love both of you as if — why, as if you were one and the same person."

"Oh, no, you don't!" I shouted. "The only person you love is yourself!"

Before she could get any closer I turned and ran up to the attic, slamming every door behind me as I passed. I didn't stop for the pots or a flashlight, but it turned out I didn't need either. There wasn't a trace of water, and the lights didn't even flicker. I stayed there, though. Partly because I was angry and partly because I was ashamed. But it only took a moment for the anger to pass, leaving nothing but dull, flat shame like puddles after a storm.

The real storm passed, too. Things grew quiet again. I looked out through the dusty, high-up window for a while, watching the clouds move south toward the city. They were dark and swarming, on an even darker sky. I love wild weather! I wished I was out there. I wished Daisy was out there somewhere, too, but Daisy was in the past.

Thinking of Daisy reminded me of the old photo albums we had looked at together. I sat down with them on the attic floor and began flipping through the pages. They were kind of a mess. Albums nowadays have pages like plastic envelopes, where you just slip things in. These were made of paper, like a book. The photos were supposedly held on by little black corners, but the corners had come unglued so a bunch of photos were in the wrong place. I tried to sort through them and figure out where they belonged.

Mostly, the photos were of birthday parties. Boy, were there a lot of birthday parties in that family! I guess there had to be, with nine kids. The only ones I recognized were Margaret and her brother Edwin. I set aside the photos they were in, because it was fun seeing how they changed from year to year. One year, for instance, Edwin had switched from knickers to long pants. It was the only photo where Margaret smiled at him. In all the others, she looked mad. In one photo in particular, where she was just a toddler wearing an old-fashioned lace dress with puffed sleeves, she looked furious. Had Edwin been pinching the skin inside her elbow?

I was reaching for another album when a cold chill spread through me. An old-fashioned lace dress with puffed sleeves? Was it just my imagination, or was that dress familiar? I held it up to the light. Not only was the dress familiar, the toddler was familiar, too! Margaret in 1932 was a dead ringer for Garet in 1982.

The chill increased. In fact, I felt numb and a little dizzy as I left the attic and went down to Gratkins's bedroom. It took courage to compare the yellowed snapshot of Margaret with the silver-framed portrait of myself, but I had to know the truth. Here's the truth: it was the same child.

Now, I remember the time I fell on my skateboard and cut my knee so badly that I could see the bone. And I remember going to Gratkins's room in the middle of the night once, after a bad dream, and Gratkins was so still that I thought she was dead. When scary things like that happen, it's as if your insides drop out of you, leaving just a shell. But those times were nothing compared to this. This time, I didn't even have the shell. In other words, I had just learned that I wasn't really Garet after all.

Who was I, then? Was I the two-year-old Margaret

that Edwin held over the laundry chute long ago? When Margaret's parents saved her in the nick of time, did a copy of her slide fifty years into the future to become *me?* Were Garet, Daisy, and Gratkins all *three* the same person?

If only Daisy had stayed to help me instead of returning to the past! She might be a little sneaky at times, but she knew how to play her cards right in a crisis. What would she have advised me to do?

The answer came in a flash. She would advise me to do what she did herself: compare our fingerprints. Very quietly, in case Gratkins heard me and came up, I took both photographs to my room where I set them on my bureau, side by side. My hand shook when I opened the bottom drawer, but I forced myself to stay cool and think of Daisy.

"Daisy's hand wouldn't shake," I told myself sternly. "Daisy wouldn't chicken out."

There's no need to go into detail. From a distance when you're not paying attention, all fingerprints look the same. But when you actually compare them, it's not hard to notice differences. Ours didn't have many. There was the scar where I cut myself last summer, naturally. Gratkins had some scars, too, and Daisy's prints were smaller. But the patterns were the same.

Gratkins walked in while I was staring at them. "What are you doing?" she demanded. "Why were you gone so long? How bad were the leaks?"

I'll never forget the look on her face when I held up the photos and the fingerprints. I would have expected it to be angry, or guilty, or scared. But it was just very, very tired.

"So you know," she said.

There were a lot of things I had meant to say. Scornful things. Hurtful things. I meant to ask why she'd been lying to me all these years, and I probably would have, except the lights went out. Suddenly Gratkins and I were in total darkness. But she was close enough to put her arms around me. So I didn't say anything at all.

Chapter 17

I've heard that most people panic in a blackout. Not me and Gratkins. For us it's like a party, and we both relax. So when the lights went out this evening, we groped our way down to the kitchen where we lit candles and improvised a supper of sardines on soda crackers, followed by cold, canned chicken soup. I know that sounds disgusting, but believe me, it was good.

What's more, it was fun. I kept getting the giggles, and Gratkins actually laughed once or twice. It was a relief, seeing as she hadn't cracked a smile since Daisy disappeared. I got her to tell me about the April day eleven years ago when she heard crying in the basement and went down to find an angry toddler in an old-fashioned lace dress with puffed sleeves.

"How did you know who I was?" I asked.

Gratkins admitted that she hadn't known at first. "After I got you calmed down, I was going to call the police."

"What made you change your mind?"

"The dress," she said. "Our initials were embroidered on the pocket: M. A. And naturally, after that I went up and looked at the old photographs."

For once, Gratkins wasn't mad at me for asking questions. I must have asked a million of them, mumbling through bites of cracker with sardine. Who wouldn't ask questions after finding out they weren't who they'd grown up thinking they were?

"I don't remember a thing about it!" I said. "Wasn't I scared?"

Gratkins shook her head. "Just angry. At Edwin, I assume. But you weren't frightened, even though you were bruised up a bit. You were a brave little thing back then, and you stayed that way. I wonder why growing up in my own time made *me* so timid?"

"You're not timid!" I protested. "And I don't think I'm very brave. Not as brave as Daisy, anyway."

Gratkins looked surprised. "You don't think much of yourself, do you, Garet? You've already told me you're not as pretty as Daisy, nor as smart. Now it's 'not as brave.' I had no idea you were lacking in self-confidence. Or are you just being coy?"

I took offense at *coy*. It's a prissy word that no one uses anymore. Not at Whetstone, anyway. By the time I finished telling Gratkins what I thought of it, she was laughing again. "You're smart *and* brave if you can stand up to me that way," she said. "You're pretty, too, but I won't waste my breath trying to convince you. Just so long as you stop thinking I love Daisy best."

We were quiet for a while after that. Both of us remembering Daisy, I guess. And both of us missing her. I didn't exactly blame Gratkins, but I couldn't help thinking that if I'd known who I was, I might have stopped Daisy from going home.

"Why did you keep it a secret?" I demanded. "You told Daisy who she was, so why didn't you tell me?"

Gratkins shrugged. "I got into the habit of not telling you, I suppose. When you were little, you might have told your teachers, or your friends. It would have made quite a stir."

"Dream on!" I said. "No one would have believed me."

"It wasn't worth putting to the test. So I fixed my own birth certificate for you, changing 1930 to 1980. It was easy — two strokes of the pen, and a three looks like an eight. Your parents are also *my* parents. And Daisy was right, by the way. I never married."

Even by candlelight, I could tell she was blushing.

"Does that matter?" I asked.

Gratkins said it mattered to her, and it was obvious she meant it. I felt sad all of a sudden. She was sixty-three and had never married, and she minded. Would the same thing happen to me, and would I mind, too?

"Why didn't you marry?" I asked. It sounded odd the way I put it, so without thinking, I added, "Who didn't you marry?"

"You ask too many questions!" she snapped, just like old times. Then she softened and said it was someone her parents didn't approve of, so she postponed marrying him until he tired of waiting and married someone else instead.

"Is he still alive?" I asked.

"I'm not sure," said Gratkins. "If so, he's quite elderly. He was a good thirteen years my senior, you know."

"I *don't* know," I said. "It doesn't matter though. Either he's dead or he's much too old for me."

Gratkins laughed. "Well, no one's asking *you* to marry him!"

"Aren't I you?" I asked. "Don't I have to do what you did?"

That made her sober up again. "Yes, you're me. So is Daisy. But times have changed, and young people have changed, too. You and Daisy needn't make my mistakes."

I shrugged. "Daisy isn't here to make mistakes."

"But if she were, they'd be her own mistakes," Gratkins insisted. "Different from mine, and different from yours. Because you and Daisy are different from me and from each other."

The more I thought about this, the more it troubled me. After giving the last sardine to Laptop and licking the salt off my fingers, I told Gratkins that she wasn't making sense. "How can we be different? We were the same baby way back at the beginning, weren't we?"

She frowned down at her lap and was silent for a long time. When she spoke it was heavily, as if she had to drag each word up a steep slope of hard reasoning. "The way I see it, we started out the same way, with what was — I don't know — in our cells. Then for a while our families influenced us. Daisy and I had large families, but all you had was me."

"So I'm different, but if Daisy had stayed, she'd grow up to be you?"

Gratkins shook her head. "We get what we were born with, and then we get our upbringing. But after that, we're on our own. So the three of us are all different from each other. Not just our personalities, but physically too. Look at our shapes! You think you're overweight. Well, Daisy is too thin. But you're both already taller than I am. Did you ever think of that?"

I hadn't. She was right, of course. Daisy and I both had to bend a little to hug her.

"And that's not all," Gratkins continued. "Take school, for instance —"

Suddenly I caught on. "You and I like math. Daisy hated it, though. You like the whole of shepherd's pie, but Daisy and I used to split up the meat and the potatoes. I'm good at soccer, but Daisy wasn't. Daisy was neat, but you and I are messy. Right?"

"Wrong!" said Gratkins. "*You* make the mess in this house. I'm the one who cleans it up. And remember when Daisy scored that goal? She could have been better than you, with practice. Remember, girls didn't play soccer in my time."

"There you go again," I said. "Playing favorites!"

We looked at each other and for a moment I thought we were going to burst out laughing. We didn't, though. It was funny, but it wasn't quite funny enough. Because there was still something missing. Or rather some*one*.

"So we're what we make ourselves," I said,

feeling sad again. "If only Daisy knew, she might have stayed."

Thank goodness the lights went back on just then, or we might have had a real sobbing session. Instead, we blew out the candles and carried our dishes to the sink.

"Do we need to do them now?" I asked. "I'd like to bring my autobiography up to date before I go to bed."

Gratkins said we could leave the dishes as long as we put all the food away. I was putting the crackers in the pantry cupboard when I looked at the family yardstick on the door, and suddenly this stupendous thought came into my head.

"But Gratkins — Daisy grew!"

Gratkins raised her eyebrows. "Grew? Well, why not?"

"She grew two inches in just four months after she got here," I explained. "But look at the pipe! *You* didn't grow that much in a whole year."

It was true: from 1943 to 1944, Margaret Atkins grew about half an inch.

"Modern nutrition," Gratkins reminded me. "We didn't eat as well. So what?"

I was so excited that I began jumping up and down. "Remember how you said Daisy had to be exactly the same in order to merge with Margaret? Well, she won't be. She grew taller, and she put on weight. I remember now, she said her party dress was too tight under the arms. So when Daisy went back, she didn't fit!"

I thought Gratkins would be excited, too, but she

just looked exhausted. "It's after ten, Garet. You may be right, but I don't see what we can do about it. We'll talk about it tomorrow."

Talk? Just *talk?* Not if I have anything to do with it! Tomorrow I'm going to climb up that laundry chute and look for Daisy.

Chapter 18

Gratkins is weird. During yesterday's storm she worried that Daisy would be struck by lightning, but it didn't bother her one bit to send me out to look for her. This morning it was my idea to look for Daisy. But what did Gratkins do? You guessed it: she said no.

"Today is Saturday," she announced cheerfully when I came down for breakfast. "What do you say we drive into town and do some Christmas shopping?"

"Sure," I said. "As soon as I get back."

"Back from where?" she asked, as if she had forgotten what happened last night. When I reminded her about going up the laundry chute, she said, "It's not safe, honey. Why, we're not even sure it would work."

"It worked for Daisy," I reasoned. "She went up that chute and we never saw her again. That proves she got back to the past."

"It proves no such thing," said Gratkins. "The

flap was open at the top. She could have snuck downstairs again and run away."

"Okay," I said. "So if it doesn't work, I'll sneak downstairs and go Christmas shopping with you."

She still said no. "What if you slip and break your leg? What if you fall and break your neck? What if you merge into Margaret and never return to 1993?"

"What if I bring Daisy back for lunch?" I asked.

She seemed to waver a little.

"At least I won't get struck by lightning," I promised. "I might even stay warm and dry."

A smile twitched the edges of her mouth.

"Chicken!" I grinned, and I went to change my clothes.

Why change my clothes? Because I was going to 1943, of course. And I had seen enough old photos to know that back then, kids — even boy kids — didn't go around in boxer shorts over long-johns with a Grateful Dead sweatshirt on top. But what should I wear? If I climbed out into Edwin's birthday party, I should at least dress like a guest.

This wasn't as easy as you might think. Jeans were out, for instance. Gratkins had often told me how most girls didn't go around in jeans until the fifties. No, it would have to be a dress. What dress, though? I consulted the photo albums for inspiration. Then I rummaged through a couple of old trunks. I was looking for another frilly dress like Daisy's, but I didn't find one. I found a couple of good skirts, however. By the time I had finished putting my costume together, this is what I wore:

1. A pleated, plaid wool kilt (it came down to mid-calf but according to the photos, it was supposed to).
2. A white cotton blouse with a rounded collar. The blouse had yellowed, but that didn't matter because it was covered by
3. A green angora sweater with four moth holes in it, which also didn't matter because they were covered by
4. A matching green angora cardigan.
5. Ankle socks (these were mine, but socks are socks) and sneakers (mine, too, since the penny loafers in the trunk were much too small for me).
6. It seemed improbable that girls back then cut their hair an inch above the ear on one side and an inch below it on the other, so I covered my head with a scarf tied the Russian peasant way with the point down my back and the knot under my chin.

Boy, did I ever look silly! Gratkins must have thought so too because when she caught me sneaking down to the basement, she burst out laughing. "Just where do you think you're going like that?" she demanded.

I said, "To 1943."

She inspected me doubtfully. "I would have worn lipstick with that outfit. Or would I? Thirteen is a little young. Maybe back then, my mother would have made me wipe it off."

"Well, you decide," I said. "What would be right for Edwin's party?"

Gratkins shut her eyes, frowned, and touched her left forefinger to her brow. This would be her facial think-hard outfit, if she had a list like Daisy. Then she moved her hand down to cover her partly open mouth with three fingertips and opened her eyes again. The facial great-idea outfit, I assumed, but I was wrong.

"What makes you think you're going to Edwin's party?"

I thought she was referring to the fact that I wasn't invited. "I've worked that out," I assured her. "If anyone but Daisy sees me in the house, I'll say that —"

Gratkins interrupted me. "Honey, you won't be going to Edwin's party. You'll be going back to your own time."

I stared at her, unbelieving. How did she figure that?

"If Daisy went back to hers, you'll go back to yours," she explained. "It figures. There won't be the slightest risk of your merging with baby Margaret — that's my only consolation. But what good can you do?"

This was such terrible news that at first I was mad at her. "How do you know? Who made up these rules, anyway? How come you know so much about it when you're the only one of the three of us who hasn't been down the chute?"

She just smiled, and I guess what I said *was* funny. Because logically, she had been down that laundry chute twice: in summer of '43 when she was twelve, and in spring of '33 when she was only two.

Gratkins was right. What good would come of reasoning with a toddler? Even if she listened to me instead of screaming for her mother, what would I say? I could just imagine the conversation:

Garet: "Hello, little cutie!"
Margaret: "Waaah!"
Garet: "Don't be scared. I have a message for you. When you grow up to be a great, big, teenage girl, I want you to come home to the future, because Gratkins and I will be waiting for you there. Can you remember that?"
Margaret: "Whaaa?"
Garet: "Oh, it's easy! You just jump down the laundry chute."
Margaret: "Mamaaa!"

Seriously, how could I get to Daisy — thirteen-year-old Daisy — and persuade her to come back to us?

"You can't," said Gratkins.

"But I have to!" I said. "What if I leave her a note? It'll say, 'For Margaret: Do not open until you are thirteen and your nickname is Daisy.' I can write all that stuff about how you are what you make yourself. She'll have to wait eleven years before she reads it, but for us it would only be a matter of hours. Minutes, even."

"Forget it," said Gratkins. "The Margaret who read that note wouldn't know who we are. She would

160

never have lived in the future. She'd think it was a joke — Edwin's joke, maybe. The last thing she'd do would be slide down the laundry chute."

So I changed back into my jeans and a sweater, and we went Christmas shopping after all. I can't say it was much fun. The weather was against us, for one thing. Dreary, December weather — damp and cold. They were playing Christmas music at the shopping mall, but it was the generic kind where "Jingle Bells" blends into "O Holy Night" and you don't really notice there's music at all until suddenly it drives you crazy. There was a Santa at every corner, and every single one of them wanted money. As for me, all I wanted was my sister Daisy, and everything I did or said reminded me of her.

"What do you want for Christmas?" I asked Gratkins.

Before she could answer, I remembered asking her the exact same thing about her birthday. Her answer had been for me to live in harmony with my new sister.

"Never mind!" I said quickly. "Whatever I buy has to be a surprise."

"What do *you* want?" Gratkins asked.

I opened my mouth to give the usual answer: my own laptop computer. Then I remembered that I already had Daisy's. See what I mean?

"We should buy a little something for your teachers at school," said Gratkins. "We do that every year."

"Why not skip Mrs. Magorian and save some money?" I suggested.

When it comes to certain subjects, Gratkins is humorless. "Where's your Christmas spirit?" she demanded. "This year especially, when she taught both of you —"

So it went. We both tried to avoid the issue that concerned us most: Christmas without Daisy. We both were unsuccessful.

"I don't care!" I said at last. "I'm going to get her a present anyway."

Which is why we left the mall and drove to the warehouse on Mount Pleasant Street, where I bought a flowery, flouncy pillow sham for Daisy's canopy bed.

I cried most of the way home. So did Gratkins, although she tried to hide her tears behind a pair of sunglasses. Sunglasses on a day like today? Give me a break! Nevertheless, I admire Gratkins. She's cool. What's more, she's smart and brave, and even fairly pretty for an old lady of sixty-three. If I grow up to be like her, I won't complain.

There will be one thing different, though. When I grow up, I'll be an author. How do I know? Because of something Leon Priner said — that's how. Remember when Mrs. Magorian asked how he created a chilling aura of suspense, and he answered that the suspense was already there and he felt obliged to write about it? Well, that's me. Lately, whatever happens, I have to write about it. So when we got home today I came straight upstairs and set up Daisy's laptop.

Except I didn't just sit down and write. First I wanted to go back to the beginning of my autobiography and read everything I've written so far. And I only got as far as the final draft of chapter one when I noticed something that absolutely blew my mind.

Here's where The Intelligent Reader says, "Hey, wow! Garet Atkins is going to *reveal all!*"

Don't get your hopes up. It's nothing that you didn't know before. But if you do a little simple, mental arithmetic, you'll understand. To help you, I'll print it once again:

BE FIFTY YEARS AHEAD OF YOUR TIME!
ACME SUPERIOR HOUSEHOLD PRODUCTS
GIVE YOU A NEW LEASE ON LIFE!

The key word is *fifty*. Gratkins and I knew that I arrived fifty years after the year when I was two, and Daisy arrived fifty years after the year when she was twelve. What we didn't think of was the *day*. Daisy left the past on July 24, which is exactly the date she arrived in our time. Edwin held me over the laundry chute in the spring of 1933, and according to Gratkins, I arrived here in April.

The point is, I bet it works the same in the other direction. Daisy left again on December 2, 1993, so she landed on the same date fifty years earlier. Today is December 4. If I climb up the chute, I'll only be two days later than Daisy.

When I climb up the chute, I should say. Because that's precisely what I intend to do as soon as I print out this chapter. Why print out the chapter? For Gratkins to read in case Daisy and I don't come back. No one really knows how the magic works. No one knows the rules. All along, the three of us have just been guessing.

Chapter 19

The big problem with an ongoing autobiography is that The Intelligent Reader knows I lived to tell my own tale. You may have been in suspense at the end of chapter eighteen, but not too much suspense. Because it's pretty obvious that I got home again unless

1. Gratkins wrote the end, or
2. I took the laptop with me to the past and died there, but the manuscript survived.

However, if you're tempted to switch to the story of how Priscilla Perry married a love-crazed horse, ask yourself this: what happened to Daisy? Stop reading now and you'll never know.

So picture me changing into those old-fashioned clothes again and sneaking down to the laundry room. Then picture me climbing inside the chute and testing Daisy's rope. I may be slim and mature, but I still have a few pounds on Daisy. What's more, I didn't trust her knot.

It was dark in that chute, especially after the first couple of yards. Dark and stuffy. At least it was narrow, so I could lean against the back while I worked my way up the front. The chute was on a slant, thank goodness. I don't think I could have climbed straight up. As it was, I nearly chickened out. I would have, if it hadn't been for Gratkins.

"Garet!" she called. "Garet, honey, I need you!"

Her voice echoed, frail and anxious, upstairs in our big, old, empty house.

Did I feel sorry for her and come out? Wrong! I felt mad. Mad that someone so nice who cared so much about two thirteen-year-old girls shouldn't have them with her, safe and sound. From then on, I didn't hesitate. Holding tight to the rope, I inched my way higher and higher. It was hard, lonely work. That chute smelled bad, and as I suspected, there were cobwebs everywhere. They kept getting in my nose, but I couldn't brush them away. I needed my arms for climbing. Especially after I got a cramp in my left calf.

Another annoying thing: my own breathing was too loud. It rasped in my ears as if I were being pursued by some beast out of a horror movie. And you guessed it, I got scared. Imagine being scared of your own breathing! But there was nothing I could do except go back or go on, so I went on. Believe me, it took forever. The ceilings are high in our house. It's a long way from the cellar up to the second floor.

But after a while, things began to change. The

smell, for one thing: it wasn't as rank and stale. And I heard voices again. Children's voices, and footsteps in the corridors.

"Edwin? *Edwin!*"

There came a shriek of laughter, and a door slammed. Was I imagining things, or could I see just the faintest glow above my head? A moment later, the glow widened into a flash of light as something dropped onto what, considering my position, I guess you'd call my lap. Don't ask me what it was. I don't want to know. It was wet and it stank, that's all I can say. It was also small, a fact for which I was grateful at the time. When were *you* last grateful that something small, wet, and stinky fell in your lap? The key word is small. Anything larger would have sent me tumbling right back down to the laundry room.

"Edwin!" someone called again.

The voice was loud and clear. I must have reached the second floor, but now what? This was no longer an empty house. Nine children lived here. Plus their parents. Plus — what had Gratkins told me? — a cook, and a maid named Lena? When I climbed out, I was likely to meet someone. I hoped it would be Daisy.

By the time I had wriggled past the flap into the linen closet, I was not in great shape. The palms of my hands were blistered. A scrape on my ankle oozed blood. I was covered with dust and who knows what else.

To make things worse, everything around me was sparkling clean. For as long as I can remember, Gratkins has used the linen closet shelves for storing

Christmas ornaments, tools, and shoe boxes full of old financial records. She keeps sheets in there, too, but not very many of them. What sheets we own are mainly on our beds. These shelves held stack upon stack of sheets. Plus bath towels, linen guest towels, tablecloths — you name it! Each stack was neatly folded and, without exception, white. I didn't want to mess anything up, so I edged out into the corridor before giving myself a shake.

There were voices quarreling in the room that in 1993 would be mine. Should I crack open the door and find out who they belonged to? Better not. Better hide. But where? Familiar as I was with the house, I felt disoriented. How different it seemed from the one where I grew up! It was as if our house was half dead while this one was alive. The corridor floor was polished, for one thing, with a long strip of carpet down the center. Each lamp bulb wore a little hatlike shade. Pictures hung along the wall, and the window over the landing by the stairs was heavily curtained, blocking out the light.

Behind the curtains — that's where I'd find shelter! I hurried toward them, but when I pulled them apart, I was so startled that I forgot to hide. It was growing dark outside, but I could see well enough to notice that the streets had vanished, and so had the house next door. There were no lights from cars or streetlamps or from other people's windows. No matter which way I looked, I saw nothing but trees and sky. To me it was a little dreary, but now I knew what Daisy had meant when she said she was homesick.

And that's how I got caught: staring out the

window. Because suddenly the door to my future room flew open and out came a boy. He was up to no good — I could tell by the devilish look on his face and the sneaky way he moved. Pulling the door quickly shut again, he locked it and dropped the key into his pocket. Then he turned and saw me.

Don't get me wrong, this was not a *little* boy. He was taller than me by several inches. Fifteen or sixteen, I'd guess. Dark hair, dark eyes, slim. Gawky around the knees and elbows, but self-assured all the same. His mouth fell open when he caught sight of me. He shot an astonished glance at the locked door, then looked back at me and raised an eyebrow.

"Holy smoke!" he said.

I tried to run. In fact, I had taken several steps before I stumbled into someone who was coming up the stairs. A woman shrieked and cried, "Margaret!"

There wasn't a doubt about it; she meant me. Grabbing my elbow, she hurried me down to the dining room, scolding as she went.

"You naughty girl, scaring me like that! What on earth are you doing here?"

"Just what I was about to ask," said the boy, who kept pace with us.

"You're a fine one to talk!" the woman snapped, turning to glare at him. "I've been calling and calling for you. The soup will be stone cold, and the others are all waiting. Who would have thought a son of mine could be so thoughtless? And it's Lena's evening off!"

The boy answered smoothly, but with a touch of malice. "I came to tell my sweet sister that it was suppertime."

My mind reeled. Who were these people? Did they really think I was Margaret? If so, where was the *real* Margaret? And where was Daisy?

The woman switched her attention back to me. "What are you doing home so soon?" she demanded breathlessly. "I thought you'd be away until Sunday night. And what in goodness' name have you been doing to your clothes? Never mind, you can change them after supper. Oh, dear, what a mix-up! Lena will have to set an extra place before she goes. Run and tell her, Edwin."

Edwin? Was this my older brother, Edwin? Then the woman must be my mother! I suppose I should have recognized them right away, but living people are different from old photographs. Besides, I was hardly in a cool, collected state of mind. What if I really *was* Margaret now? What if Gratkins had been wrong when she said we had to be identical in order to merge? What if Daisy and Margaret and I had become one girl again?

Don't laugh. It would be bad enough staying in the past forever. Staying in the past while remembering what it felt like to be Garet would be a lifelong nightmare. No wonder Daisy had been homesick! I was homesick already at the very thought of it.

Luckily, something happened to set me straight. After a place had been set for me between two kids that I guessed were my little sisters, I sat down and had a go at that soup. It was lukewarm, not cold, and it tasted good. So good that my bowl was half empty before I noticed what you might call a chilly silence.

"Whoops!" I said, putting my spoon down fast. "Did I do something wrong?"

What I did wrong was forget to say grace. This was already reassuring because the original Margaret wouldn't have forgotten a thing like that. And when I took my scarf off, there was no doubt left at all.

It was my father who commented on the scarf. He was a quiet man in a double-breasted suit who sat at one end of the table. My mother sat at the other, with nine of us kids in between. Edwin was the oldest, and then me. Looking around, I counted five little girls and one boy. There was no telling what sex the kid in the high chair was. Maybe another boy, since back then, people dressed baby boys in blue. Everyone but the baby was staring at my head.

"Would it be indiscreet to inquire as to the significance of your headgear, Margaret?" my father drawled.

Significance of my headgear? This man talked like Mrs. Magorian!

"It's just a scarf," I said.

"Then you can just remove it," said my mother. "No hats at the table."

I didn't dare argue that a scarf is not a hat. The point was, what was *underneath* the scarf: Garet hair or Margaret hair? Had Margaret worn her hair long and curly like Daisy's the day she arrived in 1993? If so and I was Garet, I was in trouble. But if I kept the scarf on, I was in trouble, too.

"There's one slight problem," I hedged.

My father's eyes twinkled. This was a good sign;

maybe I was a favorite with him, and he'd let me keep it on. "Allow me to venture a guess," he said. "You treated yourself to a permanent wave while you were visiting your friends, and you regret the fatal step."

Did this man always talk like someone in a book? The perm was a good idea, though. My mother had one. Her hair had been crimped into little ripples that seemed plastered to her scalp. In my opinion, she's the one who should have been wearing a scarf. Chances were I didn't have a perm, though. What should I do?

In the end, I had no choice. "Remove it, Margaret!" my mother said again, and I could tell that she meant business. So I removed the scarf, and without even reaching up to feel my hair, I could tell it wasn't long and curly and that I hadn't had a perm. The only kind of hair that could make my sisters giggle and my mother gasp with horror was hair cut an inch above my ear on one side and an inch below it on the other.

Looking back, the whole scene baffles me. Even after she grew, Daisy was shorter than I am, right? To say nothing of thinner and prettier. Daisy was Margaret until she was twelve. Logically, if I didn't look like Daisy, I didn't look like Margaret either. Then why didn't this family guess that I was a fraud?

Because it was so unlikely — that's why. At least, that's what Gratkins thinks. Who could be bothered to impersonate a thirteen-year-old girl? And in a family of nine kids, according to Gratkins, you don't get as much individual attention as when you're an only. So even though Margaret hadn't been gone for more than a day or so, and even though she came home taller and not so pretty, with a weird haircut, her family accepted her.

Not the whole family, though. Not Edwin. He kept his eye on me the whole way through supper, and there was no mistaking his expression. He knew something fishy was going on and meant to find out what it was. Meanwhile, he looked at me mockingly.

What did I do? I stuffed my face. This may sound insensitive, but I had several reasons:

1. In a family where you don't wear hats at the table, for sure you don't talk with your mouth full. In other words, I couldn't answer questions.
2. Who was to tell where my next meal came from?
3. The food was good, and
4. I happened to be hungry.

There were a lot of forks at my place, but they didn't scare me; Gratkins may have sold most of our silverware, but she taught me all that nonsense about starting at the outside and working in. I only made one mistake, and it had nothing to do with forks. It had to do with the way I ate the main dish, which was pork chops with peas and applesauce. Have you guessed what I did wrong? Here's a clue: I had prepared a scrumptious mouthful of sauce over meat with three peas on top when Edwin made his crack.

"Have a look at the princess, Ma! She's eating normally for once."

The scrumptious mouthful stayed where it was, kind of frozen halfway between my plate and my mouth, while Edwin got scolded for drawing attention to the much needed improvement in my finicky attitude toward food. It served him right! It seemed wiser not to stay improved, however. From then on, I did a Daisy. In case you don't remember, that means a nibble of pork, followed by a taste of applesauce, followed by one pea. I even wiped my fork on my napkin between the sauce and the pea. I should have known that Daisy brought her attitude with her from the past. She couldn't have gotten that weird overnight. Not unless she hit her head on her way down the laundry chute.

While I ate, I checked the place out. The furniture, the table settings, the pictures on the wall. Also my parents and the other kids. Gratkins would want a full report when I got back. *If* I got back. Which I wouldn't attempt to do until I found Daisy. Because if I hadn't merged with Margaret, Daisy hadn't either. With luck, she was somewhere in the house.

You won't believe this, but with all those kids, no one was expected to help with the washing up! I started to stack plates and collect the silverware, but Lena gave me a shocked look that changed my mind in a hurry. I was kind of disappointed because helping out would postpone my next big problem: where should I go? If I went into the living room, I'd have to deal with questions. I could go to my own room, of course, but which was my room in 1943?

Once again, I had no choice. The minute my parents disappeared, Edwin hustled me back upstairs and along the corridor until we were outside my future room again.

"Hustle a feisty kid like Garet Atkins?" The Intelligent Reader asks. "Give me a break! Garet simply is not the hustlable type."

True. With one exception. When someone pinches the skin inside her arm above the elbow, Garet goes where that someone asks. Boy, does it ever hurt!

"Okay, okay!" I said when he let go. "Has anyone ever told you you're a bully?"

"Yes," said Edwin. "My sister Margaret. Who are you?"

Now, I had never met this Margaret. Not thirteen-year-old Margaret, I mean. But all of a sudden I felt sorry for her. Daisy and I don't let ourselves get pushed around. The Margaret who stayed behind shouldn't either. I decided to teach Edwin a lesson.

"I *am* Margaret, you jerk! I've changed, is all. New haircut, new personality. No more Ms. Nice Guy!"

He looked puzzled. "Mizz who?"

I searched for another way to put it. "What I mean is, you better shape up or I'll make this house too hot to hold you. You'll be dead meat. Road kill. Got the picture?"

Pulling the key from his pocket, Edwin unlocked the door to my future room. "Come on, who are you really?" he asked.

"I'm Margaret," I repeated stubbornly.

"Oh, yeah?" he said, shoving me inside. "Well, join the crowd!"

Chapter 20

The joke was on Edwin, of course. It wasn't Margaret inside that room. Daisy sat on the bed in her peach-colored party dress which, like my skirt, was smudged and torn. She looked a little smudged herself, for that matter. I guessed she had been crying. She cheered up when she saw me, though.

"Garet!" she exclaimed. "What are *you* doing here?"

"I came to bring you home," I said.

Remember how I thought I'd have to persuade her? Well, I was wrong. At the mention of home, Daisy smiled for the first time in days.

There was only one small problem: Edwin. In my relief at finding Daisy, I didn't notice him follow me into the room. He had heard every word and wasn't about to let us leave.

"You two aren't going anywhere," he said. "You'll wait right here while I get my parents."

I heard the key turn in the lock again. I heard his

footsteps running down the corridor. I heard his voice yelling, "Ma! Dad!"

Daisy moaned. "What are we going to do, Garet?"

"We're going to play our cards right," I informed her, reaching inside the neck of my moth-eaten green sweater. "Edwin's not the only one who has a key."

I would have liked to stay a while. To look around the room, for instance. Daisy had never told me it was hers before it became mine. And I wouldn't have said no to a quick tour of the house. But we hadn't a minute to spare. By the time we had unlocked the door and shut ourselves into the linen closet, footsteps were coming back upstairs.

"Quick!" I said, holding open the flap to the laundry chute. "Don't try anything fancy. Just slide."

Daisy hoisted herself up, but once she was balanced on the rim of the chute, she hesitated.

"I'm scared, Garet! You go first."

If I went first, would she follow? It wasn't too late for her to change her mind. After all, I hadn't explained yet how she could be herself instead of growing up like Gratkins.

"No, you!" I urged her. "Hurry!"

Daisy's seat edged forward, but her hands still held tight. A door opened and shut, out in the corridor.

"What's that?" she whispered.

"People looking for us, dummy. Let go!"

"No, I mean that voice. Don't you hear it? Listen!"

I listened. At first I didn't notice a thing except

for footsteps in the corridor. Then I heard Gratkins calling up the laundry chute from half a century away.

"Home!" came the ghostly echo. "Come home — home — home!"

Daisy's face lit up. She kind of twisted around where she sat on the rim of the chute. And with a reckless look in her eyes, she let go. What did I do? Well, here's what I should have done if I had any sense: wait until she reached the bottom before following. And here's what I did instead: I dived in after her, headfirst. Want to know how we landed? In a pile — that's how. Me on top in my plaid kilt and moth-eaten sweaters. Daisy in the middle in her peach-colored party dress. And Gratkins on the bottom groaning, "Girls! Girls!"

I'd like to think that Daisy came home for me as much as for Gratkins. Maybe she did, but I'll never know for sure. And I guess it doesn't matter, now that we're all three together again.

But don't stop reading yet. It's still not the end of the story. First we got hugged and scolded and scrubbed and stuck with Band-Aids from head to foot. Then we got soup and sandwiches.

"I already ate, fifty years ago," I told Gratkins.

Gratkins said, "Don't get fresh."

"*I'm* hungry," Daisy announced. "It may be your second supper, but it's only my first."

"Did Edwin bring you lunch, at least?"

She shook her head and pulled apart the two sides of her sandwich.

"That little nerd!" I said. "Let me guess: he starved you the whole of yesterday, too."

Bit by bit, Daisy's story came out. When she went back to the past on Thursday morning, her first thought was to hide. It was no longer summer outside the window, she explained. She wasn't sure how long she had been gone.

"I didn't even know for certain that I was Margaret again. I hid in the attic, and late that night I snuck down for food. It was spooky!"

"I'll bet it was," I said.

Scraping the mayonnaise off the bread and depositing it on her plate, Daisy continued. "Yesterday it was different. There was still no sign of another Margaret, so I thought maybe we had joined together again. When no one was looking, I went back to my room."

"And Edwin found you there?" Gratkins prompted.

Daisy shook her head. "My sister found me there. My *real* sister, that shared the room with me. Then she went and told Edwin."

"I don't get it," I said. "You thought you were Margaret again, right? Everything was aboveboard, so why did you let him lock you in your room?"

Daisy placed the two slices of bread on the mat beside her plate. On the plate itself she had laid out the lettuce leaf, the pickle, and the slice of turkey breast. Nothing touched.

"It all gets mixed up again in your stomach, you know," I reminded her.

Daisy ignored me. "Margaret was visiting friends. She left Wednesday, and she wasn't expected back until Sunday night."

"So? She could have changed her mind and come back early, couldn't she?"

"That's what I told Edwin. The problem was, he'd just talked to her on the telephone. So he went straight to the phone to make sure, and talked to her again. And that's not all. Remember what Gratkins told you about the dress? My mother tore it up for rags, back in July. So when Edwin saw me wearing it, he knew something was wrong."

I nodded. "But why didn't he tell his parents?"

"He was going to," Daisy said. "But I was scared that once they knew about me, I'd never see you and Gratkins again. So I tried to bribe Edwin. I said I came by magic, and I'd tell him about it if he left me alone for just one minute in the linen closet first."

"And he wouldn't agree?"

"He wanted to be in there with me. That's what we were quarreling about when you arrived. Only I didn't know it was you. I heard Mama call you Margaret, so that's who I thought you were."

"But I am!" I told her excitedly. "I mean, not just my name — I'm the same Margaret as you and Gratkins!"

I began to explain, but she interrupted me. "I guessed that," she said in a calm voice. "I had a lot of time to think while I was locked in my room. I remembered what you said about turning up in an old-fashioned dress with the piglet in your pocket."

Digging into her own pocket, Daisy drew out three china animals. Then she leaned across the table and lined them up in front of me: a boar, a piglet, and a sow, all facing the same direction. "You weren't lying after all," she said. "I'm sorry I broke the piglet, but here's the one that stayed in the past. Now you can have the whole family."

"Gosh, do you really mean it?" I said.

There was an awkward pause before I added unwillingly, "I guess you should have your laptop back. And your canopy bed, of course."

Here's a test for The Intelligent Reader: which was Daisy's answer?

1. "Oh, no! I wouldn't *dream* of accepting them. I feel really bad that I didn't share them in the first place, but now they're yours."
2. "Thanks, Garet!"

If you have even the slightest doubt what Daisy said, you should be reading Staci Farnham's autobiography, not mine. Remember when Mrs. Magorian asked about moods? Well, now that I'm near the end, I can tell you what my mood is: realistic. Staci's is nauseating.

"Oh, well. I'm glad you're back anyway," I said.

"Friends again?" asked Daisy.

"Friends," I agreed. "Sisters. You name it."

Gratkins was in seventh heaven. Practically crowing with delight, she offered to read our horoscope.

"Spare me!" I said, but does Gratkins pay attention?

"Scorpios should put cold water on the flames of romance today," she reads. "Social graces win you new friends, but it's a poor time for gaining financial backing."

I laughed. "So what's new?"

Just when I was congratulating myself on the three of us being back to normal life, we heard the noise: a hollow rumbling behind the wall, like an indoor avalanche. Laptop growled, and his hackles rose. Daisy and I both froze. As for Gratkins, she just bit into her turkey sandwich and mumbled calmly, "Could that be another Margaret coming down the chute?"

Daisy and I may be a little weird, but Gratkins is downright crazy!

"Another Margaret!" I exclaimed. "And you sit there chewing?"

I held my breath, hoping she was wrong. Not that I'm selfish or anything. We live in a big house, and there's plenty of room for another kid. Nevertheless, I couldn't help thinking how many months it had taken me to come to terms with Daisy. Would I have the patience to go through it all over again?

But Gratkins was right. Partly right, that is. Someone had come down the laundry chute. Someone was stomping up the cellar stairs. Someone flung open the door into the kitchen and stood there grinning. Only it wasn't Margaret.

So now there are four of us. You know what, though? I'm not sorry. I always *did* wish I had a brother.

Afterword

You're probably wondering what happened next. When I read to the last page of a book, I always wonder what happened next. And don't expect me to fall for the "happily ever after" line, because I don't buy it, not even for princes and princesses. *Especially* for princes and princesses. So here's what happened next:

1. Edwin obviously couldn't go to Whetstone Academy, so Gratkins enrolled him in the local high school instead. This was great for Daisy and me, for reasons I won't explain, but I'll give you a hint: not one of them wore a skirt.
2. Gratkins moved my old bed into Edwin's new room and bought me bunk beds instead.
3. Staci Farnham eloped with a love-crazed duke.
4. Daisy ended up giving me the laptop after all. She decided her way of being different would be piano lessons. So Gratkins called up the music shop on Mount Pleasant Street, and we finally

have a piece of furniture in our empty dining room: a rental-purchase piano.

5. Ardeth Shaeffer won the prize for the best auto-biography. Mrs. Magorian was disappointed in the short-and-sweet version of mine. The first five chapters showed promise, she explained, but it got a little flat and boring toward the end. She was nice enough to admit that it wasn't my fault, though. She said that so far, I seemed to have lived a flat and boring life. I didn't mind too much because

6. I won the "Earth, Our Garden" prize with my story about New Pork.

7. Edwin and Daisy and I are planning a trip together down the laundry chute. I can't wait to find out what life is like in 2043!

Mrs. Magorian says that The Professional Author always leaves The Intelligent Reader with a question in his mind. Here's a question for yours. One of the things I just listed isn't true. Which one?

"Number three, of course," says The Intelligent Reader.

Wrong! So start thinking.

About the Author

ANNE LINDBERGH was the acclaimed author of numerous middle-grade and young-adult novels that take ordinary children into extraordinary situations. Her writing has been described by *Publishers Weekly* as "acutely perceptive and graced with disarming humor." The daughter of Charles and Anne Morrow Lindbergh, she lived in Vermont with her husband, Noel Perrin. Anne Lindbergh died in 1993.